Her Secret Amish Admirer

HER SECRET AMISH ADMIRER

A COZY MYSTERY ROMANCE

BETH WISEMAN

THORNDIKE PRESS
A part of Gale, a Cengage Company

Thorndike Press® Large Print Amish Fiction.
The text of this Large Print edition is unabridged.
Other aspects of the book may vary from the original edition.
Set in 16 pt. Plantin.

LIBRARY OF CONGRESS CIP DATA ON FILE.
CATALOGUING IN PUBLICATION FOR THIS BOOK
IS AVAILABLE FROM THE LIBRARY OF CONGRESS.

ISBN-13: 978-1-4205-2984-5 (hardcover alk. paper)

Published in 2025 by arrangement with Beth Wiseman.

Print Number: 1 Print Year: 2026
Printed in Mexico

GLOSSARY

ach: oh
boppli: baby
daed: dad
danki: thank you
Englisch: those who are not Amish
fraa: wife
Gott: God
gut: good
haus: house
kaffi: coffee
kapp: prayer covering
kinner: children
lieb/liebed: love/loved
maedel/maeds: girl/girls
mamm: mom
mei: my
mudder: mother
nee: no
onkel: uncle
Ordnung: unwritten rules of the Amish
rumschpringe: running around time for

teenagers prior to baptism
sohn: son
wie bischt: hello/how are you?
ya: yes

Secret Admirer

Someone who shows fondness for a person but keeps his or her identity a secret from that person.

Chapter 1

Sadie Miller was about to leave the one-room schoolhouse where she taught when she noticed a letter-sized envelope on her desk. *Sadie Miller* was written in cursive on the front. How had she not seen this earlier?

Hmm . . . most of her students only knew how to print.

She picked up the envelope, turned it over in her hands a few times, then set it back on the desk, deciding to read it after she'd readied the room for the next day.

Sadie had received lots of private notes from students over the years, and most of them weren't good news. Priscilla Stoltzfus had gotten pregnant after barely turning fifteen when she reached out to Sadie in the eighth grade. Sadie had counseled Priscilla and convinced her to tell her parents, and she eventually did. Another younger student had confessed to stealing candy from the general store. Sadie had accompanied him to the store to apologize, but she didn't tell his parents, and the clerk didn't either. Sadie suspected the young boy didn't have an ideal home life, and she sensed that the store employee felt the same way. There were so many other letters from students, and she'd read them all, often re-reading the sweet words from those who said she'd made a positive difference in their lives. She might not have children of her own, but she was helping to mold some of those in her temporary care.

She rearranged the children's desks back into straight lines, edging them slightly with her leg, then she began to close the windows in the small building. As she breathed in the aroma of flowers blooming, freshly cut grass, and the earthy smell of a recent rain shower, she thanked God for this beautiful spring day.

As was her routine, she straightened up her desk and sorted the children's work by grade. She loved the variety of projects that each age group brought forth. That's how it was teaching grades one through eight in the same room.

Sadie could still recall her Amish schooling, which only went through the eighth grade, and not much had changed. Reading, writing, and arithmetic, along with

English and German, were still producing fine young scholars.

She sat on the wooden chair behind her desk as she reflected on her education. She could still recall walking into this same schoolhouse for the first time, knowing only a few English words. That was still the case with her newcomers who had been taught Pennsylvania Dutch at home. There was a challenging excitement for the little ones to start learning a second language. The older children were fluent in their native Dutch dialect but spoke English quite well by the time they graduated. She gingerly ran a finger across the mysterious letter, still not ready to face whatever the contents might reveal.

Glancing at her calendar, she sighed. Today was April 2nd. On May 1st she would say goodbye to her eighth graders, most of whom she'd taught since the first grade. It was hard not to get attached to the students.

Sadie's biological clock ticked faster as each year passed. She was twenty-seven, and all the women Sadie had grown up with were married and had families. Past generations would have considered her to be an old maid, but Amish teens and young adults were waiting longer to get married. Sometimes, they waited for the right person, and other times, they took advantage of their running around time for as long as they could. In the 'good old days' — as her grandmother used to say — boys and girls got baptized and married shortly after their *rumschpringe,* which began at sixteen. It was a time for young adults to venture out into the world and for parents to look the other way while their children decided whether to be baptized into the faith. Sadie hadn't taken advantage of that time in her life. Her father wasn't on board when it came to looking the other way.

When she got older, Sadie was courted by many of the men in Montgomery, Indiana, but none were a good fit. She lived in a small district, so most prospects had been exhausted. Sadie wasn't sure any man would be right for her, or that she could ever trust a man not to be like her father.

She shivered at the recollections of her childhood. School had been her safe place. Maybe that's why she'd become a teacher, a job usually passed down to someone younger as each new teacher found her soulmate, a term Sadie didn't believe in.

If that had been the case, her father wouldn't have professed his love for Sadie's mother, then beat her repeatedly. Sometimes, they were physical assaults. Other times, her mother's wounds were emotional, but neither were ever in plain view for anyone to see. Sadie was an only child, and while her father had never laid a hand on her, she knew he would if she told what went on behind closed doors. Everyone saw the Millers as the perfect little family of three. Some of the women were envious of Sadie's mother. Since she only had one child, she had more freedom and less chores. *If they'd only known . . .* Even though both of her parents were deceased, the images of what went on in her house still haunted her.

Sadie stood, pushed in her chair, then loaded her seventh graders' assignments into her black satchel. She'd curl up in bed later this evening with a cup of meadow tea and grade papers following her devotions. If she finished early enough, she'd get back to the romance novel she was reading. She might not believe in soulmates and true love, but she devoured the fictional stories about a life she sometimes longed for but didn't trust.

Sadie missed her mother and often wept for the life Rebecca Miller had lived. Sadie prayed to God often that He would overlook her inability to forgive her father, since she didn't miss him at all. She pushed the thoughts aside and was about to leave when she remembered the letter.

Might as well get it over with.

She pulled out her chair, sat, and slid a finger along the seam of the envelope. She unfolded the crisp white paper and read the message:

Dear Sadie,

You sparkle like twinkling dew on a crisp spring morning as rays of sunshine light up the strands of your golden blonde hair that often escape from your *kapp* and brush against your ivory skin. You are so beautiful, and I think about you all the time.

Lieb,

Your Secret Admirer

Sadie blinked her eyes a few times before she re-read the letter, her mind congested with confusion. She held the white piece of paper with one hand as she tapped a finger to her chin, trying to recall if they'd had any adult visitors today, particularly men, who might have slipped this onto her desk.

Nee. A student must have put the note on her desk, and Sadie was in new territory. This would be considered advanced writing even for her eighth graders, even the few who could write in cursive. She thought about her older students out of the twenty-four in her class, and she couldn't think of one boy who would write something like this, an inappropriate admission of love for his teacher. Then she did remember a student having a crush on her several years ago, but he was in second grade, and it was harmless.

She had another thought. Did one of the widowers of a student send it with his child to give to her? A shiver ran the length of her spine. If that was the case, it felt a little . . . creepy.

Why didn't her admirer sign his name?

Chapter 2

Later that evening, Sadie graded papers and sipped warm meadow tea atop her covers in her bedroom. With her windows open, a nice breeze cooled the room, an owl screeched in the distance, and crickets chirped as if having a party right outside her window — sounds that usually didn't bother her — but when all those noises mixed with the tangled thoughts in her mind, she couldn't focus on her seventh-graders' work.

She turned the round knob to raise the flame in her lantern, which was on her bedside table, then reached for the cause of her distraction. After she re-read her mysterious letter three times, she pushed her work to the side and opened the drawer of her nightstand, retrieving a pad and pen. *I must list the possibilities.*

Tapping the pen against the blank page, she pictured the twenty-four children she taught daily. How many of them had fathers who were widowers or who weren't married? One of those children could have slipped her the note on behalf of his or her father. She shuddered, still finding it unsettling that a man would choose to send her an anonymous note, claiming to be her secret admirer. But she lived in a small community. How hard could it be to figure out who her mystery man was?

Lloyd Stoltzfus. She wrote his name down first, even though she didn't see him as a likely contender. While their people were encouraged to remarry soon after the death of a spouse, they were still expected to mourn for more than a month. Annie had tragically died in a buggy accident nearly a month ago, and Lloyd remained visibly upset, barely able to keep from crying during the past worship service. Sadie had known Lloyd all her life, and he wasn't what she would call traditionally good-looking, but kindness had a way of making a man like Lloyd incredibly handsome. He was a small fellow, shorter than Sadie — who rose to a height of five-foot-nine — and he had a dark beard with wavy hair the same color. But it was obvious that grief consumed him, and it was doubtful that he was harboring a secret crush on Sadie. His child, Miriam, was in first grade and mourning the death of her mother also. Sadie had caught her several times wiping tears from her eyes while at the playground as she sat off to the side not participating in a game of kickball or socializing with the other students. Sadie paused, briefly feeling the loss that Miriam and her father had suffered as she recalled her mother's funeral. But she needed to move on.

Paul Lantz. He was an outwardly handsome man with light brown hair streaked with blonde highlights from his time in the sun without a hat. It was uncharacteristic for an Amish man not to wear a hat. Sadie, along with most of the women in her community, believed Paul intentionally broke the tradition while working the fields — and sometimes in public — so that his hair would, indeed, shine with sun-struck radiance. Paul's eyes were a dazzling shade of green that twinkled with hues of gold, but behind the glistening gaze Sadie saw cat eyes, always on the prowl.

Despite his good looks, Paul had yet to take on a wife, so he didn't have a beard. It was rumored that he was more interested in activities that should be reserved for marriage, thus having scared away the previously eligible women in their district including Sadie — assuming she had been in the market for love. And while he wasn't a father, he had custody of his brother's child, Adam, a fourth grader. It was a surprise to everyone when Paul's brother and his wife fled the community to live with the English, especially since they left their only child behind. And, with Paul . . . of all people.

Sadie thought it was unfortunate that Adam was being raised by his Uncle Paul, a man who strode around with an air of vanity that took away from his attractiveness. She could see those qualities surfacing in Adam. The boy flirted with the older girls in ways that were often inappropriate, attributes that she suspected he learned from his uncle. Sadie had disciplined the boy numerous times, usually by taking away his recess time. She put a star by Paul's name as a possibility. She'd refused his advances in the past, but having his nephew slip her a note sounded like something he might do.

Sadie startled when her cell phone rang. The bishop allowed her to have a phone since she was single and living alone. The usage of mobile devices was supposed to be for emergencies only, which caused Sadie's chest to tighten, until she saw who was calling. It was Lizzie, an elderly woman who was co-owner of The Peony Inn Bed and

Breakfast. The woman had always been a rule-breaker, of sorts, and called sometimes just to chat, possibly about a new recipe she was serving guests at the inn, but mostly to inquire why Sadie hadn't married yet. If Lizzie found out about Sadie's mysterious letter, she would think she had won the lottery, a practice that was frowned upon, although Lizzie had been known to buy lottery tickets on occasion. Lizzie and her sister, Esther, loved to play matchmaker, and Sadie had been on their radar for a long time.

"Lizzie, is everything all right?" Sadie waited, suspecting everything was fine, but anxious for confirmation just the same.

"*Nee,* everything is not all right." Lizzie groaned, the type of guttural sound that Sadie had heard before from her elderly friend. An indication that Lizzie was okay but irritated about something. "The recipe you gave me for that cheese ball was horrible," Lizzie said. "Now, you know how much I think of you, and that you'd never deliberately let me serve *mei* guests something that made them gag." She hissed, in the playful way that Lizzie often did. "I'm going to read you the ingredients because I think you made a mistake when you told me the recipe." This had happened before, and Sadie was pretty sure that Lizzie had heard her wrong. Lizzie never wrote down recipes, citing a memory as sharp as a twenty-year-old, even though she was pushing eighty. Sadie waited as Lizzie cleared her throat. "Two and a half blocks of cream cheese, half a small onion chopped up, four ounces of blue cheese, one cup of cheddar cheese, and salt and pepper to taste. That's what you said." That sounded right to Sadie. "And once the balls are formed, then you roll them in pecans, parsley, and chili powder."

Sadie gasped, then slapped a hand to her mouth to keep from laughing. "*Nee* . . . not *chili powder.* You roll them in paprika, along with the nuts and parsley."

Lizzie was quiet before she sighed. "*Ack,* well . . . both spices are red. And never mind. I've got to go explain to *mei* guests what I did wrong on the appetizer. They're afraid to eat the entrée."

"A mistake anyone could have made." Sadie tried to picture her beloved cheese balls, a family recipe, rolled in chili powder. It made her stomach roil just thinking about it.

"You take care, now. Sorry to have bothered you."

Lizzie hung up before Sadie had time to

say that it was never a bother to hear from Lizzie. Her elderly friend received what she needed and that was that. Smiling, Sadie resumed her search for some clarity. *Moving along . . .*

Joseph Yoder. Sadie didn't really know Joseph. He was new to Montgomery and had arrived four months ago from Pennsylvania. He was also a nice-looking man with dark hair and a beard, both speckled with a hint of gray. Joseph was tall and built like a man who wasn't afraid of hard work, but he didn't strut the way Paul Lantz did. Joseph's details were sketchy. Sadie had heard that he ran into legal troubles in his home state, but the few times she'd spoken to him, he was polite and seemed genuinely concerned about his daughter's education and well-being. In addition to inquiring about his first-grader's academic skills, he also asked if she was socializing with other children. Sadie had noticed that Leah, like Lloyd's daughter — Miriam — stayed to herself a lot, and Sadie made it a point to spend extra time with both girls. Joseph had a mysterious air about him, in Sadie's opinion. He'd obviously been married at one time, thus the beard. Maybe he was her secret admirer.

There was only one more possible candidate who might have written the note.

Henry Bontrager. The thought of Henry pursuing Sadie romantically did cause her heart to flutter a little even though she wasn't interested in marriage. Henry had never been married, and he didn't have any children, but he was the groundskeeper for the school. He made sure they always had water, especially when it was freezing outside. Henry maintained the yard around the schoolhouse and performed maintenance on the building. He was a general handyman who worked for a lot of people in their community. Henry had a key and access to the school, which meant Sadie had to include him on her list. Maybe he had put the note on her desk earlier that morning, and she hadn't seen it until she was packing up to leave.

Henry was well-respected in their district, and while love can come along at any age, Henry was older than any of the single men in their area. He was thirty-nine, twelve years older than Sadie. Henry had it all . . . good looks with a perfectly cut square jawline, broad shoulders, and the man oozed tenderness for such a stout fellow whose appearance said otherwise. Rumor had it that Henry also had a lot of money, inheritance that he'd held on to. She'd never asked him directly, but she had heard from others that Henry only worked at the school so he would have something to do.

Henry had asked Sadie out to supper years ago, and even though she'd been tempted, she had declined. He was too nice of a man for Sadie to lead him down a path with no happy ending. But why hadn't he ever married? Was he trying to win her affections again? Had he been holding out for her? Was that his real reason for working at the school, to be near her? She recalled the gentle way he spoke to her, his willingness to always help with any project, and the way his mouth curled up slightly more on one side when he smiled. *Hmm . . . maybe.*

That was it. Four men on her list of potential secret admirers; three if she ruled out Lloyd due to his grief. Having identified the only people who had a way to get the note on her desk, it felt less menacing. Even Paul Lantz, who was creepy in general, and the most likely to pull a stunt like this, wasn't a dangerous man . . . except for the women who fell under his spell. A respectable woman with responsibilities like Sadie would need to watch herself.

Sadie placed her list on the bedside table and gathered the work she'd brought home, struggling to focus. Two hours later, she extinguished the flame in the lantern before snuggling beneath the covers. As nightfall fell, she squeezed her eyes closed but shadows from the past, always looming in her mind, swirled like a tornado.

A part of her hated her father, and not just for the way he had treated her mother. Abram Miller had left his daughter mentally scarred about marriage. Sadie had seen enough to leave her wondering if all men had a dark side, the way her father did. People in their community had no idea of the abuse Sadie's mother had suffered. When Sadie had suggested to her mother that she seek help from the bishop, elders, or others in their district, her mother responded with an adamant "No" and made Sadie promise to never tell what went on inside their home. She said everyone in the community would lose respect for Sadie's father and that it would be an embarrassment for their family. It had left Sadie wondering what went on in other households. Did other families have secrets like hers?

Sadie kept her promise to her mother even after her mom died of cancer when Sadie was eighteen. She kept their family secrets but moved out of her childhood home. It was another promise she'd made to her mother, who was fearful that once she passed, her husband would turn on Sadie. Her mother had been secretly saving money, hiding it in a can she kept buried in the backyard. On her deathbed, she revealed to Sadie where the money was. Sadie had been shocked to learn that her mother had stashed away enough for her to put a down payment on the small house and five acres where she still currently resides.

She forced the memories from her mind, refilling her thoughts with the anonymous letter. After reviewing her potential suitors, Sadie's anxiety began to settle. No one on the list appeared dangerous. Even though Joseph had a mysterious past, and rumors had spread about him having legal issues, he didn't strike her as threatening. Having come to that conclusion, she couldn't help but feel flattered, although someone was going to be very disappointed in her response . . . assuming she figured out who wrote the sentiments.

One of her responsibilities for the coming week was to schedule parent/teacher conferences, and she knew who she would schedule first. Lloyd Stoltzfus — who seemed the most unlikely — then Paul Lantz, followed by Joseph Yoder. She'd work Henry into the mix somehow. One of the four men had to have written the note.

Chapter 3

Lloyd Stoltzfus . . .

Every breath Lloyd took felt like a struggle. Even normal daily routines, like getting Miriam to school, were laborious. It had been a month since his beloved Annie had passed, but it still felt like yesterday that she'd closed her eyes for the last time.

No matter his sadness, he needed to gain a level of self-control for his daughter's sake. Miriam was only six, but the loss was tremendous for her as well. Lloyd was going to have to find a way to infuse some joy into her life.

He sighed. Sadie Miller, Miriam's teacher, wanted a meeting after school. She'd already spoken to him once, concerned that Miriam spent a lot of time by herself, not interacting with the other children. Lloyd knew his behavior was transparent, and he needed to do a better job of hiding his grief for his daughter's sake.

“Pancakes or eggs to go along with our bacon this morning?” Lloyd did his best to sound cheerful as he forced a smile. “Or both?”

Miriam sat patiently at the kitchen table twirling a string on her prayer covering with her finger. His daughter shrugged as loose strands of dark hair escaped her lopsided prayer covering.

Lloyd didn’t cook a big breakfast in the mornings, instead opting for oatmeal, cereal, and sometimes even Pop-Tarts for them. This was his first effort to break the pattern they’d fallen into. “I say both.” He took the store-bought pancake mixture from the cabinet and added water like the instructions said, whisking until it looked like he thought it was supposed to look . . . thick, but not too thick. Then he cracked four eggs into a bowl to scramble, probably added too much milk, then heated the griddle on the stove for the pancakes.

“Did you know I have a meeting with Sadie after school today?” Lloyd used the first name of Miriam’s teacher, as was the custom for the Amish. A first-name basis gave familiarity, and children were still considered respectful when they used first names for adults.

Miriam stopped twirling the string on her

prayer covering as she straightened. "*Ach.* Am I in trouble with Sadie?" She'd had a year of English schooling, so she tended to bounce between English and Pennsylvania Dutch.

"I don't think so." He looked over his shoulder and raised an eyebrow. "Why? Did you do something wrong?"

Another shrug.

"I think she probably wants to talk about your studies and how you're doing." Lloyd poured the eggs in the pan and began to scramble, then when steam rose from the griddle, he poured some of the pancake mix into four circles. "How do you think you're doing in school?"

"I don't know."

Lloyd pulled out a chair and sat next to her, then leaned over and kissed her on the cheek. "I know you miss *Mamm.*" He swallowed back the lump in his throat, a knot that would be there forever. "I miss her, too, but you know she is with Jesus now."

"I know."

"And she would want us to go on with our lives, to be happy, and have fun." Lloyd knew this was a hard sell, and Miriam didn't even shrug or acknowledge the comment in any way. "We're going to be okay, *mei* sweet *maedel.*"

"Daed!"

Lloyd turned to see black smoke coming from the pancakes he'd started cooking. He jumped from the chair and waved his hand through black smoke, but the smoke alarm went off before he could get the burnt pancakes off the griddle.

He abandoned his post and scurried four feet over where the smoke detector was blaring, but even leaning against the cabinet on the tip of his toes, he couldn't reach it.

"Here." Miriam stood next to him with a broom. "*Mamm* used this."

Lloyd took the broom from her, lifted it, and knocked the smoke detector from its place, catching it with his free hand before it fell in the sink. By the time he found where to turn off the device, the eggs had joined the pancakes with their own stream of smoke.

Miriam picked up a nearby stepstool and mechanically carried it to his side, climbed two steps, then leaned over the counter and opened the window. "*Mamm* used to do this before she started cooking."

"Ya," Lloyd said. He'd seen Annie open that window before she cooked hundreds of times since they didn't have a vent. He scratched his head, trying to decide where to start cleaning up first. "*Ach,* don't you

worry. I'll get this cleaned up and do it right on *mei* second try."

Miriam raised her sweet face up at him, frowning. "There's not time today. I'll be late for school."

Lloyd ran a hand through his hair. *"Ya, ya . . .* we'll stop at the bakery on the way. That sounds *gut, ya?"*

Miriam shrugged. It was a habit she needed to break, but Lloyd recalled Annie always saying, "choose your battles." This wasn't the time for any battles. Gott, *help me.* He stared at the pans still smoldering on the stove, then tossed them in the sink, food and all. It was then that he took note of his daughter's dress. "Miriam . . ." He tried again to swallow back the knot in his throat. He could live with a lopsided prayer covering. "Your dress is inside-out."

She glanced down at herself. *"Ach."* Her eyes lifted to his. "Do you want me to go make it right?"

He wanted to tell her it didn't matter, that they'd just go back to bed, cry, and try again tomorrow. But what kind of father did that? "*Ya,* please," he said, barely above a whisper.

After she'd left the room, Lloyd sat in a kitchen chair. He'd clean the place after he took Miriam to school. He was fortunate to work out of his shop inside the barn, although not much woodworking had been going on lately.

He thought about projects he'd recently completed, which wasn't much, and something out of character for him. He'd always worked hard. Lloyd had to find some way to get back on track for Miriam's sake.

Thirty minutes later, they left the bakery and headed for school. Miriam had barely eaten half her donut when they arrived. *Not a very healthy breakfast for a growing girl.* He pulled the buggy to a stop and noticed there weren't any other buggies tethered to the rail that ran along the left side of the gravel parking lot.

"We're late, aren't we?" He was the grownup. He should have kept better track of the time. "Do you want me to walk you inside?"

Miriam shook her head as she jumped from the passenger seat of the buggy. *"Nee."* Instead of walking toward the schoolhouse, she faced him with a hand to her forehead to block the sun. "I don't have a lunch."

Lloyd fought the urge to curse, another thing that was uncharacteristic for him. He stepped out of the buggy and tethered his horse. "I better go inside with you."

He headed to the schoolhouse with Miriam shuffling along beside him. Once at the door, he could see Sadie Miller through the glass window. She pointed at the class, said something, then threw her head back and laughed as the children began to chuckle also. It should have sounded like beautiful music. That's what Annie had always said about a child's laughter.

It was a few seconds before Sadie saw him through the glass door window and walked his way, stepping outside. "*Wie bischt,* Lloyd." She bent at the waist, smiled, and said, "And *wie bischt* to you, Miriam."

"I'm sorry we're late," he said to the beautiful Sadie Miller, her emerald eyes sparkling. Lloyd would never understand how Sadie remained single. Her looks were stunning, she was kind, and the children adored her. She would be a wonderful mother, he thought, as Sadie smiled.

"Only a tiny bit late." She pressed her thumb and first finger together, grinning until her face dimpled. "Go inside, Miriam, and take your place. I'll be right in."

Lloyd's daughter did as she was instructed, and after she'd closed the door behind her, Lloyd took a deep breath. "It's *mei* fault she's tardy." He shook his head. "A problem with breakfast." Rolling his eyes, he forced a slight smile. "As in I need to learn to cook."

Sadie tenderly touched his arm, which, despite his grief, sent a familiar sensation down his spine, bringing a wave of guilt along with it. Annie had a calming way of touching him, like the feel of Sadie's hand on his forearm now. "I understand," she said, smiling. Lloyd was glad she didn't offer up the familiar look he'd grown accustomed to . . . the one that screamed pity.

"I've received a lot of meals from those in our community, for which I'm grateful," he said, feeling a blush creep into his cheeks. "But I haven't mastered breakfast." He cringed. "And I forgot to pack Miriam a lunch."

Sadie lowered her arm, leaving a void where the familiar tenderness of her touch had reminded him of Annie. Everything reminded him of Annie.

She smiled again. "*Kinner* often forget their lunches. I keep a supply of extra food in one of the cabinets. No one will go hungry on *mei* watch." She glanced over her shoulder through the small glass window of the door before turning back to him. "I best get back to the *kinner.*" Her cheeks dimpled again. "Will we still be meeting after school today?"

"*Ya,* I hope nothing is wrong." Lloyd wasn't sure he could carry the weight of one more burden.

She shook her head, maintaining her joyful expression. "*Nee,* not at all. I just wanted to catch you up as to where Miriam is in her studies."

Lloyd nodded. "I'll be here." He gave his best effort to smile. "And I'll try not to be late."

Still smiling, she turned and went back into the classroom.

More guilt flooded over Lloyd as he watched her hips swaying, wondering if he would ever love another woman the way he did Annie. He was certain that he needed to put Miriam's needs before his own. And the fact was . . . Lloyd needed help.

Chapter 4

Sadie had set up her contenders in the order she felt she could rule them out. Lloyd was her least likely admirer. His grief was too fresh, and she could see it in his eyes earlier this morning when he'd delivered Miriam to school. But he was still one of her four suitors. Next would be Paul, then Joseph. She could address any final questions with Henry in the schoolyard when he wasn't busy.

She was tidying up her desk when she caught a glimpse of Lloyd outside talking with his daughter, who sat in the tire swing. He hugged her before entering the one-room schoolhouse.

"*Wie bischt,* Lloyd. Nice to see you again so soon." Sadie tried to speak in as neutral a tone as possible in hopes that one of the men would reveal himself without any coaxing from her. She motioned him to a chair she had placed facing her desk.

Lloyd avoided eye contact as he slid onto the wooden seat. After he removed his straw hat and placed it in his lap, he cleared his voice before lifting his hazel eyes to hers. If a person's eyes truly were the window to the soul, like her grandmother used to say, then she should scratch Lloyd off her list right now. His dark hair, square jawline, stance like a towering spruce, and smile — which he rarely displayed these days — should be enough to cause any woman's breath to catch at the sight of him. But his eyes told another story and offered an unfiltered glimpse into his heart, which clearly remained broken.

"I've-I've been concerned about Miriam." He cleared his throat for a second time, averting his eyes briefly before he looked back at her. Sadie wondered what it must be like to love someone as much as Lloyd had loved Annie. "Is she doing all right?"

Sadie laid one hand atop her other so she wouldn't be tempted to offer comfort by way of a hand on his, since he had both hands on her desk. "*Ya,* I think that all things considered, Miriam is doing quite well." It was the truth, unlike her reason for having this conference with Lloyd. "She is a little quieter than normal, but I think that's understandable. I try to keep a close eye on her."

"Is she interacting with the other *kinner*?" He raised a hopeful eyebrow.

Sadie nodded. Unlike Joseph's daughter, Leah, Miriam did mingle with the other children some of the time. "*Ya,* she jumps rope with the other *maeds* and joins in when they are all playing a game of kickball or volleyball sometimes. When I say she is a little quieter, I mean less likely to raise a hand when a question is asked." Again, she resisted the urge to touch Lloyd's hand when the man's expression soured.

"I'm glad to hear that because I feel like I am failing miserably as I try to play the roles of both *mamm* and *daed.*" He shrugged, then grinned slightly. "Like this morning's breakfast."

Sadie wanted to leave room for Lloyd to do most of the talking, and she didn't want to lead the conversation, but the sad reflection in Lloyd's eyes was tugging at her heart. "Lloyd, I think you are doing a fine job. I think a father's *lieb* can go a long way when it comes to parenting, and while you may have some challenges . . ." She paused, wondering what it would have been like to have had that kind of special love from her father. Smiling, she did reach over and gently touch his hand. "I see the way Miriam looks at you and the way she runs into your arms after school is dismissed." She wanted to add that a lot of children don't have that kind of relationship with their father. Sadie didn't know if it had always been like that with Lloyd and Miriam, or if the relationship had morphed into such a loving manner following the loss of Annie. Prior to Annie's passing, most of the interactions Sadie witnessed had been between Annie and Miriam. "I think you are doing just fine."

He glanced at her hand on his, and she quickly pulled it away, wishing she hadn't offered any physical comfort. But it felt natural for her. She thought herself to be a compassionate person. Although now, she was having trouble deciphering the expression on his face, which seemed to be a combination of embarrassment and longing as his eyes searched hers.

"I appreciate that," he said softly with eyes resembling pools of appeal, searching hers for answers. "But I know I need help. I-I just don't see myself carrying the roles of both parents." He lowered his head, then lifted his eyes to her again. "I need a *fraa,* someone loving and kind, and a woman who adores *kinner.*"

Sadie felt her jaw drop, but quickly snapped her mouth closed as her chest tightened. Lloyd had just jumped to the top of her list as the author of the letter. The man was looking for a wife. Even though it wasn't for the right reasons. Why hadn't Sadie thought about that? Despite his grief, he wanted what was best for his daughter. Sadie wasn't in the market to step into such a role, and even if she was, she feared that any woman would play a hard second to Annie. Sadie knew from her past that outside appearances could fool the masses. Her father had been a pro at doing just that. But Lloyd wasn't her father, and he was as genuine a man as she had ever known.

If he was truly in the market for a wife, Sadie needed to somehow let him know that she wasn't a candidate, but she wanted to do it with the kindness Lloyd deserved. She took a deep breath and searched for the words she needed to convey how much she cared, but without leading him on.

"Why aren't you married?" Lloyd posed the question with an unexpected air of authority. "You're beautiful . . ." He waved his arm around the room. "You clearly *lieb kinner.*" He ran his hand the length of his beard, squinting at her as if sizing her up for the position. She felt her cheeks flush at the compliment.

Sadie considered telling him the truth, that she didn't believe in soulmates or the kind of true love she'd only read about. But that could deter Lloyd from his quest for a wife, and if that's what he truly desired, she didn't want to do that. Marriage might not be for her, but it had become obvious that remarrying was on the man's mind, somewhat of a surprise to Sadie.

"*Danki* for the kind words." She smiled. "I suppose I haven't found the right man." She cringed inwardly at the white lie. Lloyd could mistake himself as that person. And when he smiled with a little less sadness in his eyes, Sadie knew she needed to backtrack. She stood abruptly, but Lloyd stayed seated.

"*Danki* for coming in to talk about Miriam. I mostly wanted to let you know that she is keeping up with her studies, despite being a little withdrawn, which I think is perfectly normal. I don't believe you have anything to worry about." She recognized the unintended sternness in her voice as if she was giving Lloyd a command.

He slowly rose to his feet and slipped on his hat, any hint of a smile gone, his expression back to the grieving widower that Sadie recognized, leaving her to wonder if she'd misread his intentions. Either way, she needed to make sure Lloyd knew that he needn't bother with pursuing her.

She recalled the anonymous letter. The words were so poetic and full of hope that someone with a lot of emotion must have written them. Still, that could be anyone.

As he thanked her for setting up the conference, there was an air of awkwardness in the room. Sadie had caused it with her stern stance.

She nodded, but her focus was on Lloyd's eyes and the recollection of his confession that he needed a wife. This meeting had not been at all what she expected.

Sadie heard Lloyd through the open window calling out to his daughter. Miriam had eventually left the tire swing and sat on the bench seat of the buggy while her father had met with Sadie, never taking the reins. Sadie's heart hurt for both, but no matter her sympathy, becoming a wife was not in her plans.

She couldn't imagine Lloyd laying a hand on Annie or Miriam.

But that's what people thought about my father.

Chapter 5

Paul Lantz . . .

Paul tucked his shirt in on the way to his buggy. "Come on, *Sohn*!" he yelled over his shoulder. "You're going to be late for school!"

As Paul untethered his horse, which he had readied earlier that morning after collecting eggs, he watched his nephew pull the door closed behind him, toting the lunch Paul had made for him.

His insides warmed as he watched the lad skip across the yard toward the buggy. Adam wasn't his son, but he couldn't have loved him any more if he was. The boy was bright, handsome like his father, and at ten years old, he was a fine student

"Can I drive, *Onkel* Paul?"

Paul nodded, unsure if he could deny the boy much of anything. His bright eyes shone with excitement as he latched onto the reins, and he seemed to see life like steady rays of sunshine always warming his soul, despite his parents running off and leaving him. Paul shook away the memories. He never would have expected his brother and sister-in-law to leave their Amish district to live with the English. And it was unthinkable that they would leave Adam, their only child. But money has a way of doing that to some people — even their people — and Paul's brother had allowed temptation to pull him from the only home he'd ever known, all in the pursuit of financial prosperity. An elderly English couple had offered Paul's brother and his wife room and board to run their farm for an unthinkable amount of money. The catch — no kids allowed. They had promised to send for Adam when they'd saved enough money for their own place, but that was over a year ago. Adam was devastated at first, but now he rarely mentioned his parents, and Paul didn't think Adam would even want to join his folks at this point. He had friends. And he had his Uncle Paul.

As the clippity-clop of hooves met with the gravel road that led to the schoolhouse, Paul breathed in the scents of spring. It was his favorite time of year. Aster, coneflowers, bee balm, and clover lined both sides of the road.

Paul wasn't much of a scholar in school, but he knew about plants and flowers. His mother had taught him at a young age, and he had fond recollections of his time with her in the garden. Paul was sure his parents would be disappointed in their older son's choice to leave the community. But if they were still alive, they would be raising Adam, not Paul. And they'd be doing a much better job. As hard as he tried, parenting was challenging.

"Why do you think *mei* teacher wants to see you after school? Am I in trouble again?" The boy's shine faded.

"*Nee,* I don't think so. It's probably just a routine parent/teacher conference." Paul wasn't sure if that was true. He worried that Adam had stepped out of line again. If so, Paul knew it was his fault. He hadn't always set the best example for the boy.

Too many times, Adam had caught him in pursuit of a woman. Once, the boy had seen him kissing Mary Francis King in his own living room before she ran out the door. He recalled the incident in his mind, unsure what he'd done wrong to upset Mary Francis. That seemed to be the way it was with the women in his district that he'd tried to court. Maybe they didn't want a man who was raising his nephew. But Paul and Adam were a package deal, and nothing would change that.

He'd even tried to court Sadie Miller, Adam's teacher, years ago. She was a beautiful woman, but she had rejected him also. That was a long time ago, when she was young and had just started teaching. Maybe things were different now.

He put his hat in his lap and scratched the scar on the top of his head. It was covered by his hair, and it wasn't unsightly, but it itched constantly, especially when he wore his hat. He'd been bending over and helping his father repair the fence when a board snapped loose and hit him in the head. He was probably around Adam's age. He'd healed up just fine, but for reasons no one seemed to understand, it had itched for years.

Adam slowed the buggy to a stop, the way Paul had taught him. "Have a *gut* day at school," Paul told his nephew. "I'll be here this afternoon to meet with Sadie, but I'm sure everything is fine." He cringed at the assurance he wasn't certain he could offer.

The boy frowned. "*Ya,* okay."

As Paul made his way around the buggy to the driver's side, he recalled his last visit to the school at Sadie's request. Adam had spoken inappropriately to a girl who was maturing physically. Maybe he shouldn't have, but Adam was only a boy, and it was hard not to notice things like that.

Sadie was on the porch greeting each child as they arrived. She was still as beautiful as ever, and it was a mystery to Paul as to why she hadn't married. He figured it was perplexing to everyone since all the men Paul knew had tried to win her heart.

He smiled to himself. This afternoon he would do his very best to steal Sadie's heart. Perhaps she had softened over the years and would be open to going out with him. Because one thing was for sure . . . Adam needed a mother. And Paul longed to have a woman to share his life with. He would square his shoulders, behave with the confidence he didn't have, and do his best to make himself irresistible. He didn't consider himself handsome, which meant he had to overcompensate in other areas. *Please Lord, help me to win over Sadie Miller.*

Sadie had sailed through the morning and afternoon, glad it was uneventful. She'd need all her energy to converse with Paul Lantz soon, and she hoped he could keep his hands to himself. Despite his good looks, the man was touchy-feely in ways that made Sadie uncomfortable. He had been reasonably well-behaved over the past few years. By that, she meant that he would wink at her or rub her arm as he passed by, but he hadn't made any real advances. She hoped it would stay that way today.

After she dismissed the children, she sat at her desk and planned out what she would say. How could she get him to admit that he wrote the note? As of today, she was confident that he was her secret admirer. Adam had randomly come up to her desk earlier in the day and whispered in her ear that his Uncle Paul thought she was pretty. Sadie had dismissed the comment and asked Adam to return to his desk.

It was tricky territory because she wanted Paul to admit to the letter, but she didn't want him to think she was open to courtship. Especially not with him.

She stiffened in her chair from behind her desk when she spotted Paul pulling into the gravel parking lot. His nephew was swinging on the tire swing outside, as Sadie had instructed him to do, so she could see him until his uncle arrived.

Paul walked over to the boy, rubbed his head, laughed, then nodded before he swaggered toward the front door of the schoolhouse, swinging his hat in his hand as he puffed out his chest. *Typical Paul.*

"Wie bischt," she said when he walked into the building.

He smiled, which women who didn't know him might find alluring. Sadie fought the urge to frown.

"I hope I'm not late," he said as he winked at her.

Sadie felt her blood starting to boil. This was not a good start to the meeting.

"*Nee,* you're not late," she said through gritted teeth. "Please . . ." She motioned to the chair on the other side of her desk.

After Paul sat, he placed his hat in his lap. He didn't even have hat-hair, meaning he probably hadn't had the hat on all day. "I hope Adam isn't in trouble and that he's keeping up with his studies."

Sadie nodded. "*Ya,* he is doing *gut* with his studies, and his behavior . . ." She wanted to tread lightly but still get answers. ". . . has been better lately."

Paul slouched into the chair and grinned like a Cheshire cat. "Then what's the reason for the visit?" He winked at her again. "Did you just want to see me?"

Sadie's chest tightened as something inside her snapped. "Paul, it is inappropriate for you to have your nephew relay a message from you — that you think I'm pretty — and it's even more unacceptable for you to send a note with him to leave on *mei* desk." She placed her palms on the desk and sighed. "Please don't pursue me in a romantic way."

It wasn't what she'd planned, but now it was out there. She held her breath and waited.

Somewhere amid her speech, Paul's jaw had dropped, and any sense of presumption had fled and left him rather pale. He blinked his eyes a few times, although they weren't twinkling with hues of gold. The man looked like he might cry.

"Paul, I . . . um . . ." Clearly, she'd hurt his feelings more than she'd intended, and the color in his face returned, morphing into a bright red. "Maybe I should have said something other than —"

He held up a palm as he locked moist eyes with hers. "*Nee,* I heard you loud and clear."

The confident Paul Lantz was wounded more than she could have imagined. Sadie lowered her eyes. "I'm sorry," she said softly before she looked up at him.

He seemed to force a smile. "It was worth a shot. And you're right, I shouldn't have had Adam do my bidding by telling you that I thought you were pretty." His smile broadened. "But you are, pretty that is."

Sadie felt her cheeks matching the color of his. "*Danki,* that's nice of you to say." She wasn't sure where to go with the conversation now. She cleared her throat. "Anyway, Adam is doing well in school. I just felt like we needed to clear up this other situation with his whispering in *mei* ear and the note."

Paul scratched his temple with one finger as he frowned. "Sadie, I really am sorry about having Adam whisper that in your ear. But I don't know anything about a note."

Sadie drew in a deep breath as she tried to calm herself. She liked to think she was good at reading people's expressions, and the look on Paul's face appeared genuine, as if he really didn't know what she was talking about.

"You didn't have Adam leave a note on my desk signed 'your secret admirer'?" Her heart pounded like a bass drum against her chest.

He chuckled. "Sadie Miller, I've known you all *mei* life. Does that seem like *mei* style?"

She thought for a few seconds. It really didn't seem like the Paul she knew, much more brazen, but also more vulnerable than she'd suspected.

He stood, placed his hat on his head, and

said, “If that’s all, I guess I’ll be going.” He turned before Sadie could respond. There wasn’t a swagger in his step anymore, and his shoulders were slumped as he opened the door and left the building.

Sadie turned in her chair and watched Paul approach Adam on the swing. He said something to the boy that caused him to smile, then Adam followed him to his buggy, and the child climbed into the driver’s seat. That wasn’t unusual since most children learned to drive the buggies around age nine or ten.

But what was unusual was Paul’s demeanor once she’d called him out on what she thought were two indiscretions. If he’d written the note, why wouldn’t he have admitted it since he was quick to fess up that he’d instructed Adam to tell Sadie she was pretty?

Maybe he hadn’t written the note. Perhaps Sadie had misread the man Paul really was for all these years.

Chapter 6

Joseph Yoder . . .

Joseph showed up right on time at the school, and he was pretty sure he knew what the meeting with Leah's teacher would be about: Leah's detachment from the other children. Joseph had seen her sitting by herself many times when he'd shown up early. Sometimes, she would be sitting with Lloyd Stoltzfus's daughter, Miriam, perhaps, because they were both suffering from the absence of their mothers. The difference was that Miriam's mother had died. His daughter's mother was alive but still gone. But maybe the girls found comfort in each other.

When Joseph questioned Leah about not making many friends, she always said she was tired. Joseph believed her. His daughter was often in bed and asleep before dark, and sometimes Joseph had to gently shake her in the mornings to rouse her. He hoped she hadn't been falling asleep in school. He'd read that sleeping so much could be a sign of depression.

His beautiful daughter was sitting on the tire swing when he arrived, not moving, and staring at her feet.

"*Wie bischt, mei* little butterfly." It was a term of endearment that had stuck since she was a toddler, his beautiful little girl who loved to chase butterflies.

"There aren't any butterflies here," she said as she looked up at him with sad eyes.

He squatted down in front of her. "It's the beginning of spring. The butterflies are on their way. They just haven't made it here yet." Leaning closer to her, he kissed her on the forehead. "I'm going to go talk to your teacher. I don't think it will take long."

His daughter nodded, and it broke Joseph's heart to see her so sullen all the time. They had been in Montgomery for four months. He had hoped some of the sting of their circumstances would have begun to heal by now. But why should he expect that from his daughter when his own heart was shattered?

"*Wie bischt,* Sadie," he said as he entered the schoolhouse, closing the door behind him.

"I'm *gut,* Joseph. *Danki* for coming in."

She stood from where she had been sitting in a chair behind her desk, her hands clasped in front of her, with a smile that would make any man stumble to get his balance. But even as her cheeks dimpled and her emerald eyes sparkled, he reminded himself of his situation and forced a stern look on his face.

"I hope Leah isn't in any kind of trouble." He held his position in the middle of the aisle, school desks on either side of him. It reminded him of the school he had attended in Pennsylvania. Sometimes he missed it there. Other times, he loathed the place. That's what happens when you run away from something.

"*Nee, nee.* She isn't in trouble. Leah is very sweet and does well with her studies." She waved an arm toward the chair in front of her desk. "Please, have a seat."

Joseph wondered what this woman's agenda was if Leah wasn't in trouble and was doing well in school. "Can I ask what the purpose of the meeting is?" He wanted to get to the point, retrieve his daughter, and go home. Even though it didn't feel like home.

He raised an eyebrow, but the teacher was still standing and had brought both hands to her chest. She seemed a little young to be having a heart attack, but something wasn't right with her. He wasn't even sure she was breathing and looked a little wobbly. "Are you okay?" he finally asked as he edged closer to her desk.

Sadie forced herself to breathe, catch her balance, and sit. "*Ya, ya.* I'm fine." She had spent the weekend keeping herself busy so she wouldn't continue to think about her secret admirer. But as she gazed at Joseph, she was practically willing him to be her suitor, which was completely out of character for her.

She'd spoken with Joseph occasionally, although he stayed to himself a lot and rarely walked Leah to the door of the schoolhouse. Even during worship services, the men were on one side and the women on another. Joseph and Leah consistently departed on Sundays immediately following the meal. Joseph was tall and muscular, but she'd never really gazed into the depths of his eyes the way she was now. *What am I sensing that I haven't seen before?*

Today, she felt like she was seeing him for the first time. He was older than she was based on his dark hair that was graying at the temples. Maybe in his thirties. He didn't strut the way Paul did, but his stance was sharp and confident. Close up, his good looks momentarily stunned her, but there was an air of isolation in his expression, as if he really didn't want to be here. Perhaps it was the mystery that surrounded Joseph that added to his allure. Folks speculated about his arrival. Did he commit a crime back in Pennsylvania? Did he have family troubles? Where was his wife? He had a beard, so he was married at one time. But he'd been tight-lipped, and no one really knew why he was here with Leah. Most likely a widower, she assumed.

She cleared her throat as she put a clammy hand to her forehead, surprised this man was having such an effect on her. But, once again, she reminded herself that men couldn't be trusted. Especially one with a past he didn't share with anyone.

"*Mei* apologies," she finally said as she tried to smile. Her insides swirled with a sensation she didn't recognize. How in the world could she question him about a secret admirer note when she could barely squeak out any words? *This isn't like me.* "Please, have a seat," she said again, aware of the shakiness in her voice as she motioned to him, the same way she'd done with Lloyd and Paul.

Frowning, Joseph sat and placed his hat

in his lap, but he didn't say anything as his eyebrow rose again.

"Um . . . Leah is doing well in her studies, but she . . ." Sadie cleared her throat again. ". . . she stays to herself a lot, and I wondered if there was anything I should know to help her make friends." She blew out a breath of relief, smiled, and was proud of herself for coming up with a direct question that might shed some light on Leah . . . and her father.

Her thoughts drifted as she realized that three of her hunches were raising children who had lost at least one parent. It was the common thread. Henry was the only one who didn't have a child factored into the scenario, and she'd catch up with him later.

"She just needs time." Joseph's expression didn't change, and he was a tough man to read, his eyes a window covering to whatever was in his soul.

"Is there a situation that I should be aware of, so that I can help her with whatever might be troubling her?" Her intent was genuine, but it was also mixed with a dose of nosiness. Now, it was she who lifted an eyebrow and waited.

He leaned forward, rested his elbows on his knees as he clasped his hands beneath his chin. *"Nee,"* he said, his eyes locked with hers, his stoic expression in place.

"Um. Okay." Sadie wasn't sure where to go from here, but as with the others, she had to know for sure if he wrote the note. Although based on his overall demeanor, she seriously doubted it.

An awkward silence ensued.

"Is there anything else?" he finally asked.

"Nee," she said as she twirled the string on her prayer covering, the same way some of the young girls in her class did when they were nervous.

He stood and put on his straw hat. "Have a good day, Sadie." His words sounded formal as heavy footsteps marched toward the door.

"Wait!" Sadie hadn't planned it, but she was on her feet, and Joseph had spun to face her. She still had not asked him about the note, but after taking a deep breath, she rethought her approach. "I-I sometimes notice Leah spending time with Miriam Stoltzfus. You might know that Miriam lost her mother only a month ago. I just wondered if maybe . . ." She bit her bottom lip.

"If her *mudder* is dead?" Joseph smirked, which seemed odd. "*Nee,* her *mudder* is very much alive." He folded his arms across his chest as he tapped a booted foot against the wood floor.

Sadie startled at the sound of his deep and stern voice, but she still hadn't asked the question on her mind. It seemed irrelevant since he just implied he was married and not a widow. But the question hung in the air like wet laundry that would never dry if she didn't ask.

"Joseph, did you write me a letter?" She squeezed her eyes closed, and when she opened them, he was peering at her, his jaw partially dropped. "Someone left me an anonymous letter, signed by *mei* secret admirer. And I'm trying to find out who it might be." Her heart thumped in her chest so hard that she wondered if he heard it from across the room.

"What?" He took off his hat and frowned as he ran a hand through his peppery-colored hair with a dash of salt at the temples.

Sadie's face was surely three shades of red, but she had to go on. "I'm asking the single and widowed men who have *kinner* in *mei* class if one of their sons or daughters might have slipped me a note on behalf of one of their fathers." She shrugged. "I find it unsettling that someone would do that."

His eyebrows narrowed into a frown as he continued to glare at her, then pointed a finger at his chest. "I'm married."

"*Ya,* I know. But I didn't know that until a few moments ago." Her bottom lip began to tremble. She disliked confrontation. "I'm sorry to have bothered you about it."

He put on his hat and sighed. "No apology necessary." Then he abruptly left the building.

Sadie turned and looked out the window, the way she'd done with the others she had interviewed about the note.

Joseph lifted Leah into his strong arms from the tire swing, and the girl laid her head on his shoulder. Even after they were settled in the buggy, Joseph's daughter leaned her head against him.

As he steered the buggy out of the school parking lot, Sadie mentally checked him off the list. *He's married.* She'd probably gotten more information out of him than the entire community had managed to do in the past four months. But his admission only led to more questions. *If his wife isn't deceased, where is she? Why isn't she with him? And . . . why all the secrecy?*

CHAPTER 7

Joseph . . .

Joseph was barely out of the school parking area when he slowed the buggy to a stop, causing Leah to lift her head. "*Daed,* am I in trouble?"

"*Nee, mei* little butterfly. You are not in trouble." He scratched his chin. *But I think your teacher might be.* He didn't want to worry his daughter, so he chose a version of the truth. "I need to go back to the school. I forgot to ask your teacher something." He had noticed the way the teacher's bottom lip had trembled. Had he caused that? Or was she afraid about the note? "Can you play on the swing for only a few minutes while I go back inside?"

His beautiful Leah nodded and even smiled a little.

After Joseph returned to the parking lot and tethered his horse, he walked to the entrance while Leah skipped to the swing.

He eased the door open. Sadie had her head in her hands but quickly looked up, blinking her eyes.

Joseph walked all the way to her desk and sat in the chair, placing his hat in his lap again. "I want to say that I'm sorry if I sounded snappy with you."

"*Nee,* don't apologize. I must sound silly, questioning men about a mysterious note." She shook her head. "I've known *mei* only suspects — for lack of a better word — all of *mei* life."

"Except me." He smiled. "But now you know that I can't be the one pursuing you, but I did think of something."

Her eyes brightened. "Really?"

"*Ya,* I was a teenage boy once." He recalled his youth, a happier time in his life. "And I did have a crush on *mei* teacher when I was in the eighth grade. Your secret admirer is probably one of your older male students." He smiled again, hoping to show her that he really wasn't a horrible guy, but someone offering a solution that might put her at ease.

She opened her desk drawer and pulled out an envelope. She offered it to him. "Do you know any thirteen or fourteen-year-olds who write like this?"

He tipped his head to one side as he accepted the envelope. "Are you sure you want me to read it?"

She shrugged. "Why not? I only have one person left to speak with, the only other man in our community who relates to the school whom I haven't cleared off *mei* list."

Joseph unfolded the letter and read silently.

Dear Sadie,

You sparkle like twinkling dew on a crisp spring morning as rays of sunshine light up the strands of your golden blonde hair that often escape from your *kapp* and brush against your ivory skin. You are so beautiful, and I think about you all the time.

Lieb,

Your Secret Admirer

Joseph's initial thought was that every word in the note was true, but then his stomach churned. "You're right. This isn't the writing of a teen or pre-teen boy." He handed the letter back. "Who is the last person on your list, the one you haven't spoken with?"

She averted her eyes from his as she blushed. "I probably shouldn't say, but since I've shared so much already . . ." She sighed. "It's Henry Bontrager, our school's handyman."

Joseph had seen the man around the property plenty of times.

"He's older than me. Almost forty, I think." She chewed on her bottom lip again. "He's very kind, the *kinner lieb* him, but he's never been married so I had to include him."

"How old are you?" Joseph usually had better manners, but the note alarmed him. The secrecy of it all. Then he realized he wasn't one to be talking about secrecy.

"I'm twenty-seven." She lifted her eyes to hers. "And you?"

"I'm thirty-four," he said, feeling like a much older version of himself ever since things had gone badly in Pennsylvania. He tapped his temple with one finger and grinned, hoping to lighten the darkening mood. "I probably look older with *mei* gray temples."

She smiled. "*Nee,* I heard an *Englisch* woman say that when men turn gray, they take on a distinguished look." Chuckling, she added, "But women just look old."

Joseph couldn't imagine her ever looking old. If he wasn't married, she would have been the only woman he would have wanted to court since his arrival in Montgomery. She wasn't just beautiful. Everyone spoke highly about her even though there seemed to be confusion as to why she wasn't married, a thought that led him to his next question.

"Why do you think Henry hasn't ever been married?" he asked.

She shrugged. "I don't know." Shaking her head, she said, "I just don't think he would have written the note."

Joseph leaned back in his chair, crossed one leg over his knee, then peered past Sadie to see his daughter. Leah had kicked the swing into motion and almost looked like she was enjoying herself. *Time. Leah just needs time to heal.*

Sadie looked over her shoulder before turning back to him with a smile. "Leah is a very sweet child."

Joseph's guilt wrapped around him for the way he'd snapped at Sadie. "And I know you are just looking out for her best interest. I appreciate that." He didn't want to draw her into a conversation about his marriage, so he regrouped. "Are you waiting around to talk to Henry?"

She nodded. "*Ya.* I'm dreading it. He's going to think I'm so silly. He's such a kind man, and I don't want *mei* questions to make things awkward between us."

Joseph knew what it was like to think you

knew someone, when they were a completely different person.

"I can stay. I mean, if it would make it easier for you." He raised one shoulder before lowering it slowly.

She laughed. "*Nee,* I'm certain that would make it worse. I'm going to embarrass the poor man as it is." Sighing, she threw her head back and groaned, then looked back at him. "Maybe I should just strike him off the list and not bother questioning him."

"But then you'll never know for sure." Joseph folded the letter, put it back in the envelope, and handed it back to her. "It seems a little creepy, an anonymous note. I'm sure everyone in your district knows each other. Why the anonymity?"

"That's the word that came to mind for me, too, *creepy.*" She scowled. "I lead such a quiet, peaceful, uneventful life. This has thrown me off kilter."

"Why aren't you married?" Joseph tipped his head to one side, keeping his eyes directly on her so he wouldn't miss her reaction.

"That seems to be the question of the day." She tapped a finger to her chin and looked away from him. "I just haven't found the right person."

Joseph prided himself in being able to spot

a lie, and the lovely Sadie wasn't telling the truth. *Someone else has a secret.*

Sadie was surprised how easily she had fallen into a conversation with the mysterious Joseph Yoder from Pennsylvania, the man everyone speculated about. But she wasn't about to reveal why romantic relationships didn't interest her at this point in her life.

"I guess you will know when the right person comes along," he said.

She forced a smile. "*Ya,* I suppose."

Joseph stared past her, his expression tight with strain. "She's going too high."

Sadie looked over her shoulder and put a hand to her chest. "*Ya,* she is." Sadie had warned the children many times about going too high in the tire swing. Three years ago, a boy around Leah's age fell and broke his arm.

Suddenly, she was reliving that moment when Leah flew from the tire and went airborne. Sadie was instantly on her feet, but she fell far behind Joseph, whose sprint and long strides had him out of the schoolhouse and reaching his daughter long before she did.

Sadie fell to her knees in the sandy area around the swing. She'd had the playground filled with sand, but Leah had fallen hard. Joseph had her in his arms in no time.

"*Daed,* I'm okay." She wiggled out of his embrace, her normally sullen eyes sparkling. "Did you see how high I went?"

Sadie willed her heart to stop beating so fast as she lowered her head and thanked God that Leah didn't seem injured. When she looked up, Joseph had tears in his eyes.

"I couldn't stand it if anything happened to you." He pulled her close again, burying his face into his daughter's small shoulder.

Sadie knew she should speak up, say something to Leah about all the reminders she'd been given about not swinging too high, but father and daughter were having a moment. Sadie had no words. Despite the circumstances, it was beautiful seeing them like this, tightly embracing each other with love spilling out the way Sadie pictured eternity to be — perfect love. Something she would never experience, with a man or a child of her own.

Leah wiggled free again. *"Daed . . ."* She cupped his face so tenderly with her tiny hands that Sadie covered her mouth with three fingers and merely watched. "I'm not going anywhere. Nothing is going to happen to me." Such maturity, Sadie thought, as she watched this six-year-old child comforting her father. But her words only brought more confusion for Sadie.

He nodded but seemed speechless, his eyes still moist. Sadie felt like an intruder in their moment, but she was relieved that Leah was all right.

Leah continued to hold her father's face between her small palms. "*Mamm* left us, but you'll always have me."

Sadie pinched her lips together to stifle a gasp. The secret about Joseph Yoder was out.

Chapter 8

Joseph's eyes darted to Sadie, and it was impossible not to see the surprised recognition on her face as her eyes widened. He said the first thing that came to mind. "Please don't tell anyone." It was a secret he feared she wouldn't be able to keep, making this place not feel far enough away from all that had imploded in his world. People would begin to talk. As it was now, he and Leah were a mystery to everyone. After folks in the community got word about Joseph's wife leaving him, he'd be outcast, gossiped about, and speculations about why Grace left would swirl around him like a tornado that would never calm.

"I won't tell anyone." Sadie spoke softly, but there was a sincerity in her voice, and a passion in her gaze, that made him almost believe her. "You have *mei* promise," she added.

Leah twisted her small body until she was

looking at Sadie. "*Mei mamm* was a beautiful person, but she lost her way. Now, me and *Daed* are alone."

His daughter's words brought forth a huge lump in Joseph's throat, which he struggled to swallow before he opened his mouth to speak, but nothing came out.

"I'm sure your *mamm* was a beautiful person." Sadie cupped Leah's cheek tenderly with one hand. "Just like you."

Joseph wanted to tell Sadie that she needed to hurry up and find the right person to marry because she would be a great mother. But he just watched the loving way that she looked into his daughter's eyes. Leah smiled again. Joseph's hardened heart softened a tiny bit more every time his daughter smiled or showed any sign of joy, especially related to a woman. It was uncharacteristic for Leah. She'd shied away from women since Joseph had separated from his wife. He was attempting to provide a better life for Leah, far away from the trauma she'd endured.

He smiled at Sadie, hoping she could read the 'thank you' he was sending her.

Sadie couldn't imagine how anyone could walk away from a handsome man like Joseph, unless . . . she brushed the thought from her mind. Everyone wasn't like her father, but he had scarred her emotionally enough to know that she could never be sure about anyone. But how could a mother leave her child? She wanted to ask what 'leave' meant exactly, but it wasn't her business.

Joseph finally stood and placed a hand atop Leah's prayer covering. "Are you sure you're okay?" His deep voice, although warm and controlled, was still infused with concern.

"*Ya,* I'm sure." Leah smiled as she lifted herself to her feet.

Joseph brushed the sand from his black pants before he took a deep breath and pointed behind him. "I need to go get *mei* hat."

He walked to where he'd lost his hat while running to Leah. After brushing it off, he walked back toward her, then looked at his daughter. "Leah, tell Sadie bye, and I need you to go wait for me by the buggy."

Leah did as she was told as Sadie wondered what Joseph had to say.

"Sadie, I realize you don't know me at all, but can we just pretend that Leah's admission about her mother never happened?" He hung his head, then looked up at her and sighed. "I know it's a lot to ask."

"I will not say anything to anyone. I gave you *mei* word."

"Danki," he said, still glowering. "I saw Henry pull up on the other side of the building. I think I should hang around to make sure everything goes smoothly when you ask him about the note."

Sadie smiled. "Chivalry," she whispered as she looked down at the ground.

"I'm sorry. I didn't hear you." He leaned closer to her.

She shook her head, surprised at herself for verbalizing the thought. "Nothing. It was nothing." She wiped the loose sand from her brown dress. "And, *nee,* it's kind of you to offer, but I'm not worried about Henry at all. He is one of the nicest people around." She half chuckled. "I hope he doesn't hate me after I ask him about this note." She covered her face with her hands and groaned. "Again, I feel silly."

When she uncovered her face and dropped her hands to her sides, Joseph cocked his head to one side. "What are you going to do if he admits to writing the note?"

Sadie hadn't considered that scenario. She had expected denial from all her potential suitors, but she had assumed she would be able to tell if they were lying. "I-I'm sure he didn't." Suddenly, she didn't know anymore, but she was certain that she didn't want Joseph present when she questioned Henry.

He raised an eyebrow. "Are you really sure? You don't seem convinced."

Sadie thought for a few minutes, then locked eyes with Joseph, knowing she needed to convince him that she would be fine. "He didn't write the note. I'm going to ask him about it just so I can be one hundred percent sure. And I'm not worried about a negative reaction at all. As I said, he is a kind man." At the very least, he'd always been nice to her and the children. But didn't everyone have a dark side? It was always possible, but not Henry.

"Okay, then." Joseph sighed. "*Danki* for keeping *mei* secret."

She nodded then turned to head back to the schoolhouse, dreading her conversation with Henry. She knew he would come inside soon to empty the trash cans and run the dust mop across the wood floors. Until then, she needed to think about how to broach the subject. She was sure it wasn't Henry, but maybe he would have some ideas about who her mystery man might be.

Henry Bontrager . . .

It had been a long time since Henry had

felt the warmth of a woman's body next to his, although leaning against the outside of the schoolhouse wouldn't have been his first choice for the experience.

He'd met Gretchen at the coffee shop earlier in the week when they'd sat and talked for nearly two hours. She was new to town, not Amish, and worldly about things Henry knew nothing about as a born and raised Amish man. But the woman — and her advances — were too much to ignore. This was the third day they'd met outside the schoolhouse during Henry's work hours and made out like teenagers. Henry had initially told her that he wasn't comfortable being physical at the place where he worked, not to mention the possibility of getting caught by Sadie or one of the children. Gretchen said it made their escapades that much more exciting.

As his body fought the temptation to betray his righteous upbringing, his sense of right and wrong skidded and skewed. Still, he managed to say, "I don't think we should do this here."

"We're just kissing," she said in a deep whisper as her breath breezed into his ear before she nibbled on his earlobe, which sent a shiver up his spine.

"But the schoolteacher could come out at

any moment," he said, although he feared he didn't have the willpower to put an end to what was about to cross a moral line. Regret would follow if Sadie, of all people, caught him in this position. He adored Sadie, and it would devastate him if she thought less of him.

Henry's last words were smothered by Gretchen's lips, soft and full, yet firm on his mouth. The heady sensation and the feel of her against him caused him to completely lose his faculties as he devoured the seductiveness of her lips and seared a path of kisses down her neck.

It was at that exact moment that Sadie came around the corner, and Henry was sure that the look on her face would haunt him for the rest of his life.

"Sadie!" his voice hitched as he held Gretchen at arm's distance. I-I just, uh . . ." What could he say? There was no explanation outside of lust that he could offer up. "I-I . . ." He lowered his arms from Gretchen as he hung his head in shame.

The clickity-click of Gretchen's high heels caused him to jerk his head up. She swung her hips in her denim pants and pink blouse, her blonde tresses bouncing against her back as she walked toward Sadie, whose mouth was still open, her eyes wild with the same shock Henry felt churning his insides.

Henry wanted to run away, to do something other than watch what was unfolding.

"Hello, I'm Gretchen," his new friend said before stopping in front of Sadie and extending her hand, as if being caught smooching on school grounds wasn't an issue.

Sadie snapped her mouth closed and slowly shook the woman's hand. "Hello," she said as she looked around the woman and glared at Henry. He flinched at the power of her expression.

Gretchen looked over her shoulder and smiled before she turned back to Sadie. "This is all my fault, not Henry's. He said we shouldn't be carrying on at the school, but he's just so adorable that I couldn't keep my hands off him."

Henry silently asked God to split the concrete beneath his feet and allow it to swallow him up. He would never live this down. And of all the people to bear witness . . . *Sadie.* Even if he hadn't gotten caught, he would carry the shame of his actions like a heavy sack of coal for a long time. He barely knew Gretchen, and it wasn't the way of his people to behave in such a manner. And if any of them did, it was much more discrete.

Sadie folded her hands in front of her. "Gretchen, could I please have a word with Henry in private?"

Henry held his breath as his heart pounded in his chest. *Will Gretchen argue?* Would she cause him further embarrassment? He knew it took two people for this type of behavior, but he just wanted Gretchen to walk away. He wasn't sure he wanted to see her again. Witnessing Sadie's reaction was enough to rethink his scandalous behavior, but would he lose his job? Would Sadie tell the elders what she had seen? His heart continued to thump at an unhealthy rate.

"Yeah, of course." Gretchen smiled at Sadie before she spun around and walked back to where Henry was still swimming in embarrassment and shame. She kissed him on the cheek. "See you soon."

He waited until the click of her shoes disappeared around the corner before he looked at Sadie. Again, he opened his mouth to say something, but nothing came out. The hum of a car motor in the distance momentarily distracted him before he turned back to Sadie.

He felt the searing glare that attached the space between them like a cattle prod to his forehead.

Chapter 9

Sadie spun on her heels and made an about-face toward the schoolhouse entrance, wishing she'd never left the comfort of her chair. She'd gotten concerned when Henry hadn't come inside long after his usual time. She heard him quickly shuffling behind her, but she didn't turn around.

"Sadie, wait," he called out. "Please."

She wound around her desk and sat as she willed her heartrate to return to normal. She'd caught people kissing before. Her people were human when it came to physical affection, but this type of canoodling — and with an *Englisch* woman — was off-putting.

Henry stood about six feet from her desk, took off his hat, and locked eyes with her. The lines across his forehead deepened, defined by his furrowing eyebrows. She'd never recognized their twelve-year-age difference more than right now. He looked older, somehow. Henry was still a handsome man with his normally bright blue eyes that appeared sunken in right now. The wrinkles that feathered from each eye were more pronounced.

Sadie sighed. "Henry . . . I'm not sure what to say." They'd always been friendly to each other even after Sadie had denied his offer of courtship years ago. She wouldn't say they were especially close, but she'd always thought him to be a kind and decent man. What she saw a few minutes ago had her questioning that. And it made her wonder if he'd written the note after all.

His expression was tight with strain. "Sadie, I am embarrassed and ashamed by *mei* actions." His lip trembled as he spoke. "I'm sorry that you had to see that."

"Me too," she said without thinking. She slouched into her chair, emotionally exhausted from the day. "Henry, I'm not your keeper. You are free to do whatever you want to do." She frowned, straightening in her chair. "But please do not do it on school property. What if any *kinner* had seen that display?"

He ran a hand through his dark hair. "I know, I know." He paused, inched up to her desk, and sat in the chair facing her. "She seemed so nice when I met her. And, um . . .

she *is* nice. But she's not right for me. I know that. I just got caught up in the moment."

Sadie waved a dismissive hand. She didn't need to hear any more. "Just not here, on school property, Henry." Now she had to decide if she would ask him about her mysterious note. The matter at hand had seemed much more pressing, but after seeing such a charade, maybe Henry was capable of more than she thought. How much did she really know about him?

"It won't happen again." Henry sighed. "I don't even want to see her again." He grinned a little. "She's too much woman for me."

Sadie's jaw dropped, and Henry's expression reflected the realization of his inappropriate comment.

"That's not what I meant to say," he said, frowning. "Carrying on in such a way with someone who is basically a stranger isn't right in the eyes of *Gott.*"

The bluntness of his comment drew her back to her own mystery, which also needed a straight-forward answer. More and more, she wondered if Henry was the one who wrote her the note. There was only one way to know for sure, but would he lie? She opened her mouth to take her chances with the question, but he spoke first.

"Sadie, can I ask you something?" Henry's expression leveled, and it seemed he had bounced back to himself, and a bit too quickly for Sadie, who was still reeling.

But she nodded. "*Ya,* go ahead."

"Why aren't you married, someone as pretty as you?" Henry tipped his head to one side, not smiling, but not frowning either.

Sadie buried her face into her hands. If one more person asked her that . . . She should have been used to it by now. It wasn't like the question hadn't been coming up for years.

She lifted her eyes to his as a fire brewed inside. "Because I don't want to get married. I don't want to date. I don't want to be courted, and I enjoy my quiet life without a man running *mei* life." She'd never been that straightforward, and it felt good. "So, any thoughts you might have in that arena should be redirected."

Henry's eyes grew round as saucers. "I'm sorry I asked." He waved a hand. "Not *mei* business." He stood, his face as red as the roses on her desk, two single stems in a white vase.

He was out the door before she could question him about her note. All her concentration had been shattered when she noticed the roses. Where did they come from? The flowers weren't there earlier.

Joseph tucked Leah into bed after reading her a story, then he kissed her on the forehead. "Sweet dreams, *mei* little butterfly." He looked down at his beautiful daughter, then silently prayed that he would be able to keep her safe for all her days. As he watched her take in a big yawn, he wondered if he had done the right thing by telling her that she had to forgive her mother. It's what Joseph had been taught his entire life, forgiveness. The fact that Leah thought her mother had left them was a hardship of their circumstances. But Joseph had no regrets. Leah was young. Maybe she would forget the events that caused this life overhaul for them.

As her eyes became heavy, Joseph extinguished the flame on the lantern he'd carried into her room, made sure her flashlight was on her nightstand, then he tiptoed to the living room and sat on the couch, kicking his socked feet up on the coffee table.

There was a part of him that regretted not telling Sadie the entire truth. But Grace was not a part of his and Leah's life, and that's all the schoolteacher needed to know. He also knew that no matter how hard Sadie tried, she'd likely break her promise to him. She would eventually tell someone that Joseph's wife had left him, presumably for another man. That part was true even though it wasn't the full truth. He certainly wouldn't tell the additional details to a woman he barely knew. Sadie would tell someone. He was sure of it.

As he pondered his situation, he concluded that he would have to disregard what people thought, which he knew would be easier said than done. For whatever reason, this was God's plan for him, and he couldn't keep running. And that part — what he was running from — would remain his secret forever. *I hope Leah will forget,* he thought to himself again. But, if she didn't, he would do whatever it took to help her heal.

It was early, but when he laid his head against the back of the couch, drowsiness set in. He was startled by a knock at the door.

Sadie had tethered her horse on the fence post before she made her way across the yard, her hands trembling as she knocked on Joseph's door. Everyone knew where he lived. It had been big news when he'd first blown into town with his young daughter and no wife.

Her chest tightened when the door opened and Joseph stood on the other side of the screen in a white T-shirt, his black slacks, and his suspenders off his shoulders and swaying at his sides. His dark hair was flat on the top from his hat.

"What's wrong?" he asked as he eased the screen open, his face drawn into a worried expression. "Are you okay?" There was no hiding his surprise that she was there.

"Everything is all right." She took a deep breath and paused, looking over her shoulder at her horse and buggy before turning back to him. "I mean, I think it is. I just . . ." She sighed and shook her head. "Never mind. I shouldn't have come."

He shrugged. "*Ach,* you're already here. You might as well come in and have *kaffi* before you go home."

Sadie didn't move.

He edged the screen door wider and motioned with his hand for her to step over the threshold. She pulled her sweater around her and stepped inside to a warmer space. Early spring still brought cool temperatures in the evenings.

"I'd already percolated some *kaffi.*" He nodded toward the couch. "Have a seat, and I'll be right back."

Sadie didn't move at first. She was too stunned by her behavior, showing up like this at a man's home she barely knew. But in a strange way, she felt like he was the only person she could trust, even if just a little.

"Cream and sugar?" he yelled from the kitchen, which made Sadie wonder if Leah was already asleep, or if he'd wake her up by bellowing the question.

"*Ya,* please," she said, not as loudly.

She slowly sat on the couch and took in her surroundings. Joseph hadn't done much with the place. Sadie had been in the farmhouse when the previous owners lived there. One white wall was still stained where they'd had a leak from a heavy sideways rain which blew water in along the pane of a window. The same brown and not-so-white square rug was underneath the wooden coffee table, and the old recliner, worn on both arms where Big Jake Hershberger used to stay, was still in the corner. One thing was different. There were about a dozen magazines on the coffee table that drew her hand to the pile. All hunting magazines, she noticed, as she flipped through them.

"I haven't had time to do much with the place," he said when he returned carrying two cups of coffee, handing her one before he sat next to her on the couch.

She cleared her throat. "You must do a lot of hunting." Her people hunted, but for some reason, she found this odd about Joseph. The man didn't look like he could kill anything. He had a gentleness in his eyes and expression. She cleared thoughts of her father again and wondered if she would always think of him, any time she thought of anything that involved violence, even hunting.

"I've killed a few deer." He took a sip of his coffee. "I'm not fond of hunting, but there are a lot of folks here who aren't excited about putting me to work. So, I've been able to process the meat myself and sell it." He shrugged. "Not sure what I'll do after I've cleared *mei* property or the deer get wise and move on."

Sadie thought about all the home improvement projects she had at her house. Contractors were backed up for months. But she didn't know this man. Again, she questioned her choice to come here.

"How did it go with Henry?" Joseph shifted his weight and turned to face her on the couch, his expression sobering. "Is everything okay?"

Sadie tucked her chin and tried to plan exactly what she wanted to say. *The truth,* she decided. After taking a deep breath, she locked eyes with him. "Remember how you asked me not to tell anyone about your *fraa* leaving?"

He scratched his cheek as his eyebrows narrowed. *"Ya?"*

"Don't worry. I didn't tell anyone, and I won't. But . . ." She sighed. "I guess I need to ask if I can confide in you the same way. I'm asking if I can talk to you about something and request that you don't tell anyone."

Joseph frowned. "Something happened with Henry, didn't it?"

Sadie set her cup on the coffee table and hugged herself, rubbing her arms even though she wasn't cold anymore. "I don't know. It was just odd, and I'm not comfortable talking to anyone in our district because I don't want people to look down on Henry."

"What did he do? Did he harm you?" Joseph's fists rolled into balls, which was unnerving and flattering in a protective sort of way.

"Nee, nee," she said as she dropped her arms, then reached for her coffee cup. After taking a sip, she told him what happened. Everything, including the roses that someone left in a vase on her desk.

"I saw those roses when I sat across from you at your desk, but I didn't know they were brought in behind your back. No one should be sneaking around like that." His jaw squared as a fire burned in his eyes. "I don't like this." He set his cup on the coffee table, seemingly oblivious that it spilled when he did so. "I mean, I realize that I don't know any of your potential suitors, but something isn't right. I can feel it in *mei* bones."

"Promise me you won't say anything to anyone." Sadie chewed her bottom lip.

He shook his head. "I won't tell a soul."

She believed him. Who would he tell, anyway? He didn't really know anyone. Another mystery about Joseph. Why did he choose Montgomery, Indiana, if he had no friends or family here?

"Something he said felt callous to me, the way he said it. He said the woman named Gretchen was too much woman for him, and he smirked when he said it." She twisted her mouth back and forth. "But he was so remorseful afterward that it's confusing. But I think the fact that he said it shocked me because I wouldn't have expected Henry to say something like that."

"What does your gut tell you? Do you think he wrote the note?" Joseph relaxed into the couch and sipped on his coffee.

"Honestly?" She rubbed her forehead as she allowed herself to settle into the back of the couch. "*Nee,* I don't."

"So, you're back to square one?" He ran his hand the length of his dark beard, resting just below his chin, and a reminder that he was married.

"I'm not sure I ever left square one." She shrugged. "There aren't any other single or widowed men in our district. I just assumed it was one of the four. But I guess I should narrow the list to three since you're married." She cringed. "I'm sorry. You probably don't like to think about that."

He shook his head again. "It's okay. It gets a little easier for me as each day passes. I'm not sure about Leah though, like how much she remembers about certain things related to Grace, her *mudder.*"

Sadie bit her lip and resisted the urge to push him for details. But now she knew the name of Jospeh's wife. *Grace.*

"And that's hard for me." He looked away, his eyes drifting to a faraway place. "She needs a *mudder.*"

Coming from any of the other men, she might have taken what Joseph said to be something that would land him back on her suitor list. But the Amish didn't get divorces, no matter what. So, one thing was for sure. Joseph Yoder didn't write her the note.

"*Danki* for the coffee." Sadie took a final sip before she set the cup on the table and stood. "I should probably be on *mei* way. I just felt like someone should know what happened, but I don't want to start a gossip fest about Henry."

Joseph lifted himself from the couch. "Are you sure you want to go? You aren't keeping me from anything. Leah has been asleep almost an hour. All I have to look forward to is a long night of nothingness." He smiled.

His face lit up when he allowed himself to display a level of contentment, and Sadie smiled back at him. "Read a *gut* book," she said.

"Do you have any?" he quickly asked as he followed her to the door.

Sadie was an avid reader. "Not any about hunting." She looked over her shoulder and nodded at the magazines on the coffee table.

He chuckled. "I wouldn't think you would. But I enjoy novels, mostly mysteries." He stroked his beard again. "Maybe that's why I'm intrigued — and a little worried — about your secret admirer."

"I don't think you have to worry." She was reconsidering an earlier thought. "You said you are having a hard time finding work. What kind of work do you do?" She swallowed hard, surprised she had reconsidered. But something about Joseph made her feel safe.

"I can do just about anything, although I've never done welding."

"If you're available, maybe come by *mei haus* tomorrow around five. I've been waiting on contractors for months, and I have several things that I need done. I have part of a fence down, a leaky faucet outside, and I'm being taken over by ants." She groaned. "And that's just for starters. If you'd like to come over and talk about what you might be able to tackle, I'd be open to that."

"You're not worried about what people will think?" His expression showed genuine concern.

Sadie lifted her chin. "*Nee,* I'm not. And, not to bring up a bad subject again, but you have a beard, so it's obvious you're married."

"*Ya,* okay. *Danki.* I can use the work."

"Okay —"

"I've got to go." He pointed over his shoulder. "I think I hear Leah upstairs."

“I hear her too. Go, go. I’ll see you tomorrow.”

Sadie retrieved her flashlight from her pocket and carefully started down the porch steps, the light at her feet. Without him watching her, she shone the light around the yard. The house might not be in tip-top shape, but his yard was lovely. The flowerbeds surrounding the house were filled with flowers just beginning to bloom, and as best she could see, had been recently weeded and mulched. He even had red . . . roses. She might not have stopped in her tracks if she hadn’t shone her light directly on a pair of gardening shears next to a full bush of blooms to her left.

After she looked over her shoulder and saw no sign of him, she inched closer and leaned down. Her heart seized in her chest when she noticed two stems, freshly cut.

Chapter 10

Joseph rushed up the stairs to Leah's room. His daughter had stopped moaning, but she lay whimpering on her bed under the covers. Joseph flipped on her flashlight and shone it at the ceiling before he gently peeled back the covers.

"And what has *mei* little butterfly so upset this evening?" He brushed back strands of light brown hair from her sweet face, then handed her a tissue from the box on the nightstand.

She dabbed at her eyes with the grace of someone twice her age.

Grace. Joseph's adrenaline spiked in an unhealthy way every time he thought about his wife and everything she'd done to ruin their lives. But was Joseph completely innocent? How couldn't he have known what was going on? And maybe he could have handled the situation better.

"I had a bad dream." Leah inched up in

her bed until she was propped against her pillow. "It was about *Mamm.*"

Joseph sighed, again questioning the way he'd handled things with Grace then and now. He had sought help from the bishop in their hometown, but since the bishop was Grace's father, that hadn't gone well. And Leah refused to talk to anyone about their circumstances.

"I'm sorry, Butterfly." Joseph fought the urge to yawn as he searched for the right words to comfort his daughter, if that was possible. "*Mamm liebed* you in her own way, but she wasn't happy with us, and that is not your fault. Nothing that has happened was your fault, and you don't have anything to be afraid about." Joseph was frightened enough for them both.

Leah sniffled. "Will I ever have a new *mamm*?"

Joseph hung his head and sighed again. "Do you want a new *mamm*?" It didn't seem possible since Joseph would be married to Grace for life, even though he never wanted to lay eyes on the woman again.

"I don't know," Leah said softly as she pulled the cover up to her chin.

Joseph needed to tread carefully. "All *mudders* aren't like yours."

Leah rubbed her eyes but didn't say

anything.

How could Joseph promise her something like that when he'd nearly been stripped of his faith when it came to marriage and motherhood? All he could do was be the best parent he could, keep his daughter safe, and make sure she grew up with a strong faith, despite what had happened.

It seemed like a stretch. Joseph didn't think he'd ever trust another woman, but he also knew that he had to put Leah's needs ahead of his own. The child needed a mother. *But how?* Joseph was married.

Sadie paced her kitchen, a cup of coffee in her hand. All this caffeine was going to keep her up tonight, even if her own thoughts didn't.

Her mind kept racing back and forth between Henry's unsettling behavior and Joseph's shears by the rose bush, two stems newly cut.

She didn't know the man and shouldn't have gone over there. But then she wouldn't have noticed the cut roses, which put him at the top of the list now.

And what about Henry? What if she'd never seen him with Gretchen? How much of his behavior had influenced her feelings about a man she thought was kind and trustworthy? And just because he acted inappropriately with an outsider, did that make him a bad person?

"Argh," she said aloud as she topped off her coffee cup.

Sadly, the two people who could probably help her sort through not only her feelings but also these different personality types — Lizzie and Esther, owners of The Peony Inn — were off limits. No matter what, she wouldn't break her promise to Joseph, whether he had landed back on the suspect list or not. And the women would complicate an already complicated situation.

The elderly matchmaking sisters would take on this challenge without hesitation. In their minds, love would be in the air just waiting to be captured. And what's more romantic than a secret admirer?

Only in their thoughts, Sadie surmised, since she still found the note disturbing.

But someone wrote it, that was for sure.

She recalled the kindness that radiated from Joseph's eyes and what appeared to be true concern about her situation. Again, she drew on her experiences growing up. An entire community had thought Sadie lived in a perfect world. How many times had Sadie doctored her mother after one of her father's beatings? *Too many to count.*

Maybe there was an innocent explanation for it all, but as Sadie saw things now, Joseph wasn't being forthcoming. When a person attempts to deceive, every possibility is up for grabs. Did he lie about the letter? It seemed too coincidental that two roses showed up on Sadie's desk, and an odd fluke that she noticed two stems missing from Joseph's bush. Was that a sign from God, a warning that Joseph could be lying?

After she showered and eased into bed, she took her notepad from the nightstand. She flipped to a new page.

At the top of her list, she put Joseph. All she had to justify his being moved up the ranks was the flowers on her desk, the gardening tool, and freshly cut roses. But that seemed like enough to make him her number one suspect, which caused her to frown. She liked him.

Next, was Henry, a man she'd known for most of her life. A person who, until today, had seemed genuine, kind, and trustworthy. But his comments and actions outside the schoolhouse had landed him in second place on her list of possibilities.

As she wrote down Paul's name, she recalled their visit and how much his reaction had surprised her. There was a vulnerable side to Paul that she hadn't known about. Maybe she'd been wrong about him on several levels, but she remained confused about his intentions, thus he was number three.

Lloyd was least likely to have written the note or left the flowers, but she still listed him as number four. His heartbreak was so evident, and maybe he was seeking out a wife if only for his daughter. But she didn't believe he could write the note or sneak in flowers.

She tapped her pencil against the pad of paper, re-reading her notes. Every time she went back through her interviews, as she thought of them, something felt off about every single one. The men had all surprised her in one way or another, but she had to consider that perhaps there was someone out there that she hadn't thought about. Perhaps a married man who fancied her behind his wife's back? She cringed at the thought, but she had to consider that it was plausible.

She took several deep cleansing breaths to calm her thoughts. Joseph would be here tomorrow evening, at her request, to discuss the projects she'd mentioned to him. If they came to an agreement about his working for Sadie, he would have to bring Leah with him. At his admission, he didn't really know anyone here, so he wouldn't be leaving his daughter with a family member while he worked at Sadie's house.

She would use the opportunity to get to know Joseph better. Especially, since he was now at the top of her list. She extinguished her lantern even though she wasn't tired. Her mind wouldn't turn off, combined with too much caffeine. But she closed her eyes and tried to replace worries with prayer. She would need to be alert tomorrow, watch for clues from any of the men, and prepare herself for Joseph's visit tomorrow evening.

Joseph waited in his buggy for Leah to meet him after school the following day. A big part of him wanted to go see Sadie, to lay eyes on her and make sure she was all right, but he would see her this evening. He was grateful that she had offered him work, and he hoped she really did have things for him to do and hadn't just taken pity on him.

His stomach roiled when Henry walked across the yard in front of the schoolhouse toting a shovel. Joseph was in no position to judge a man he didn't know, but Henry's actions had been enough for Sadie to seek out Joseph's opinion about the matter. And Joseph's current opinion was that he didn't care for the man.

He parked his buggy alongside others who were waiting on children to exit the building. Slowly, they began to pour out, mostly the older kids first. Usually, Sadie was outside holding the door open while everyone left, but Joseph didn't see her today. It was a minute later when he saw Leah running toward the buggy, and she was smiling.

Joseph's insides warmed as he watched his little girl heading in his direction, and with a bounce in her strides. Maybe it had just taken time.

She was breathless when she tossed her small backpack on the floor of the buggy and crawled inside. "*Daed,* Sadie said we are going to her *haus* tonight to talk about you fixing things at her *haus.* Is that right?"

He grinned, content that Sadie had thought to mention it to Leah. "*Ya,* that's right. Does that sound okay to you?"

She nodded enthusiastically. "*Ya,* I like my teacher a lot." Putting a hand to her forehead, an effort to block the sun as they pulled out, she asked, "You like her, too, *ya*?"

Joseph guided the buggy onto the two-lane road and gently pulled back on the reins to slow the animal down to a steady trot — and to buy himself some time. He hadn't seen Leah this upbeat in a long time. He didn't want to squash any hopes she had, but he also didn't want her to think that he could get involved with anyone. Even though Leah knew he was married, childhood fantasies were to be expected. Joseph would have never expected Leah to be hoping for a new mother after everything that she'd been through, despite what she said when she was woken from sleep the night before.

"I don't really know her," he finally said. "She seems nice."

"All the *kinner* like her." Leah glowed in a way that was refreshing, and if Sadie was the one making his daughter feel alive again, then he would embrace the joy for now. "And she never raises her voice or gets mad."

He nodded, unsure what Leah expected from him. Sadie was nice. She was beautiful. And unmarried . . . unlike Joseph.

When he pulled up to their house, Leah snatched her backpack, ran across the yard, and up the porch steps, still with the same bounce in her step, something Joseph had missed more than he'd realized.

He smiled to himself. Maybe Montgomery, Indiana, would be a place where they could make a new home and stop running from the past. He had no plans to lie to members of the community. So far, he'd managed to stumble around with his own version of the truth; that he and Leah moved here alone to start a new life. He supposed, when he listened to it in his mind, that it could sound intriguing to some folks. If everyone only knew how terrible things had been, and the bad choices he had made, they would probably run him and Leah out of town.

After he'd fed and secured the horse in the barn, he shuffled across the yard, eyeing the work he and Leah had put forth on the flowerbeds. There was nothing like getting his hands dirty by tilling God's soil, then seeing the fruits of his labor blossom.

The inside of the house needed a lot of repairs, but at least they'd made the outside look presentable. He latched on to the handrail and lifted his heavy work boots up each step, stalling on the third step when he noticed something. *A garden tool.*

He leaned closer to where the rose bushes were almost to the top of the porch, several sporting red buds. The bushes grew wildly, and he regretted not cutting them back in mid-February when they'd first arrived. As he studied them, wondering if it was too late to trim the bushes, he saw that two prickly spears were stems only. Someone had clipped two roses.

Joseph thought about the flowers on Sadie's desk before he looked at the house in time to see Leah watching him out the window.

Chapter 11

Sadie had just finished making a list of things that she needed repaired when Joseph pulled in, and she could see Leah in the passenger seat of the buggy. She stood from where she'd been sitting on the couch.

Supper hadn't been discussed, but Sadie had warmed up a beef stew she had in the freezer and prepared a salad. Her stomach had whirled the entire time she'd worked on the easy meal. Somehow, she had to confront Joseph about the flowers. She didn't want to do it in front of Leah, so when she'd gotten home, she'd found an old box of toys that used to be at the school for the children entering for the first time. She and teachers before her had let them play for a short while before settling down to work. Last year, they had upgraded the collection of toys.

Sadie had hauled the box up from the basement. Perhaps it would entertain Leah while she told Joseph that she knew about the flowers. The box would also serve as a reminder to donate the toys after Joseph's and Leah's time at her house. But for today, they would come in handy.

Sadie walked to the window in time to see Leah running toward the door.

"*Wie bischt,* Sadie." The girl threw her arms around Sadie when she opened the door. It wasn't uncommon for some of the children to hug her, but it was unusual to have a student at her home.

No matter, though. Sadie was happy to see Leah so happy, instead of mostly sullen. She would make it a point not to bring up the issue of the flowers around the girl, but she had to confront Joseph. He had to have written the letter. There was no way she could have two secret admirers. But every time her thoughts went full circle, she remembered that Joseph was married.

"Wie bischt," Joseph said as he walked into the living room and began to work his way out of his boots.

Sadie appreciated his manners but also took the opportunity to study him. His dark hair and beard, speckled with hints of gray, gave him a distinguished look. There was an inherent strength in his face, although it seemed to mask a vulnerability just beneath the surface. The clear-cut lines of his profile complemented his muscular stance. The man was incredibly handsome even with the spread of feathery lines around his mouth and near the corners of his eyes, indications that he must have smiled a lot and been happy at some point in his life. Rarely did she see Joseph smile, but when he did, he controlled the space around him. Sadie wondered, though, how much of his mysterious allure magnified his good looks.

"I smell something *gut,*" he said as he glanced around Sadie's living room, smiling slightly, but enough to send a ripple of contentment up her spine.

"Ya." She brushed the wrinkles from her black apron. "I know we didn't discuss supper, but I assumed you both would be hungry at this time of day." She glanced at Leah who had already found the box of toys and was sorting through the faceless dolls, puzzles, and books. "I brought those toys from the basement. We kept them at the schoolhouse for new students, but I bought some new things last year. I couldn't see throwing those items out, though. I should probably eventually donate them." She crouched beside Leah and reached for a faceless doll wearing a white dress with a black apron. "This was *mei* doll as a child,"

she said as recollections filled her mind with childhood memories. Some good. And lots of them awful. But she treasured the doll her mother gave her when she was around Leah's age. "I named her Grace."

Leah dropped the book she'd picked up and lowered her head. It took a few seconds for Sadie to realize her mistake. *Leah's mother's name is Grace.*

"But, um . . . you can rename her if you'd like." She glanced up at Joseph. He wasn't exactly frowning, but his eyebrows had furrowed with a look of concern. "Sorry," she mouthed in his direction.

He seemed to force a smile as he looped his thumbs beneath his suspenders. "It's okay," he whispered.

"Who's hungry?" Sadie stood and hoped her stew might mitigate the awkward start to the evening.

Leah lifted herself to her feet, but the twinkle in her eyes upon arrival had vanished. Sadie could have kicked herself for making such a mistake. Leah had to miss her mother terribly, no matter the circumstances. *What kind of woman leaves her child? Especially such a beautiful little girl.*

After they were seated at the kitchen table and had prayed silently, everyone loaded up with stew, and Sadie's hopes came to fruition. Father and daughter came to life, smiling and delivering compliments on the food.

"Danki." Sadie felt herself blush. "I do a lot of baking for others, but I don't often have guests over for meals." She scrunched up her face. "If I'm being honest, I must tell you that I had this in the freezer and warmed it up."

"I'm happy to eat anything in your freezer." Joseph grinned, then winked at her, which took her out of the moment and back to the letter and roses.

She lowered her eyes to her bowl, spinning the soup with her spoon. "There's plenty in there." Maybe she was a little glad that he was most likely her secret admirer, which was silly since he was unavailable. Courtship wasn't an option for either one of them. If her assumption was correct, it also made him a liar since he had adamantly denied writing the note. Sadie wished she could calm the whirlwind of thoughts swimming around in her mind and just enjoy having company for supper.

Leah ate all her soup, then asked if she could be excused to go play with the box of toys in the living room. After Joseph nodded, Sadie said, "*Ya,* of course." Then she turned to Joseph, whose bowl was empty. She swallowed back the lump in her throat and took a deep breath. "If you're done eating, can we go sit on the porch? There's something I need to talk to you about."

He wiped his mouth with his napkin before laying it across his plate, his bushy eyebrows furrowing again. "*Ya,* there's something I would like to speak with you about as well."

Sadie took in a slow breath as she wondered what was on Joseph's mind.

"Can I help you clean this up first?" He motioned to the table as he stood.

"*Nee, nee.* I'll get it later." She wanted to get this awkward conversation over with.

He waved an arm for her to go ahead of him, then he stopped in the living room. "Leah, Sadie and I will be on the porch chatting if you need anything, *ya*?"

The child nodded, but Sadie noticed the doll — Grace — was across the room. Again, Sadie chastised herself for telling her the doll's name.

Outside, the sun hung low in the sky. Sadie suggested they sit in two of the four rocking chairs on the front porch. Even with only a few visitors, she'd found the set of chairs at a resale shop in town, which lent warmth to the porch space.

"You have a nice place here," Joseph said

as he sat, then crossed one foot over his knee.

"Danki." She shrugged. "It's small, and I only have five acres, but that's plenty for me to tend to."

Joseph had put his hat back on when they exited the living room. Sighing, he removed it and put it in his lap. "I know you said you needed to talk to me about something, but I think I better go first." He scratched his cheek before blowing out a long breath. "Mine is . . . um . . . awkward."

Sadie couldn't imagine anything being more awkward than her telling him she knows he brought the roses from his house, then confronting him about lying about writing the letter.

"*Ya,* okay," she said softly as her heart pounded in her chest.

"I think I know who put the roses in the vase on your desk." He leaned his head back, closed his eyes, then looked directly at her. "Leah," he said, frowning.

"What?" Why hadn't Sadie thought of this? Was Leah in the market for a new mommy? Relief washed over her. "I-I can see why she might do that." She paused. "I mean, I think. But what about the letter?" *Or is Joseph not telling the entire truth?*

Joseph chuckled. "*Ach,* Leah isn't old

enough to come up with a note like the one you received. But it appears you have two secret admirers, and one of them is *mei* daughter. I saw the garden clippers and two clipped stems." Pausing, he seemed to be gazing at the stars as nightfall came. "I know she likes you, but in general . . ." He turned his attention to Sadie. "She isn't very trusting."

Sadie nodded, not wanting to get too nosy, but curious why Grace had left Joseph and Leah. She cringed before locking eyes with him. "I'm so sorry about telling Leah that the doll's name was Grace. I didn't even think about it, and —"

"Nee, nee." Joseph waved her off. "You shouldn't apologize. I've been working with Leah on ways to help her adjust to her mother being gone. She's going to hear that name. She's going to hear other *kinner* talking about their mothers, and she's going to have to get used to the void in her life." He shrugged, frowning. "It's not like I can replace her *mudder.*"

Sadie chewed on her bottom lip and wondered how she could have thought Joseph was the letter writer. Not only did he not seem the type, but he was married — a fact that kept slapping her upside the head, like a reminder not to get close to him.

Sadie didn't plan to get close to anyone even though the swirling in her stomach when she was around Joseph said otherwise sometimes.

"What did you want to talk to me about?" Joseph finally asked.

"Uh, actually the same thing." She crossed one leg over the other and settled into the rocking chair, less nervous than before. "I saw the two roses and the clippers when I left your *haus*." She veered her eyes away from his, but she caught him smiling out of the corner of her eye.

He pointed at her, grinning. "You thought it was me? You thought I gave you the flowers? But . . ." He paused. "Do you think I'm lying about writing the note?"

Maybe it was the sincerity in his voice or the way he was looking at her. Perhaps it was the romantic backdrop of a setting sun and no clouds in the sky . . . but she believed him.

"*Nee*, I don't," she said, meaning it. "I had to consider it before you told me that you knew Leah had cut the roses."

He laughed. "You are a popular lady."

Sadie smiled. "I like to think I'm popular with the *kinner*. Since I'm not planning to have any of *mei* own, they are the next best thing." She jerked her head in Joseph's direction and received the expression she'd known was coming. *Why did I say that?*

"But, why? You're so *gut* with the *kinner.* Leah is proof of that. Like I said, she isn't very trusting since her *mudder* left."

There it was again — her mother leaving, void of any follow-up explanation.

Leah pushed open the screen door. "I'm thirsty," she said meekly, not looking at her father or Sadie, and staring at her bare feet as if she were afraid to pose the question. "May I have something to drink?"

Sadie rose right away. "Of course, you can have something to drink." She looked over her shoulder at Joseph, assuming they'd both said their piece, although Sadie wished Joseph would have shared more about his background. "Ready for dessert?" she asked as she pulled the screen door open.

"*Ya,* sure." He stood and followed her in his socked feet to the living room, then Sadie and her guests went into the kitchen.

Sadie motioned to the kitchen table. "Have a seat." She quickly cleared the dishes from earlier and put them in the sink, then she opened the refrigerator while Joseph and Leah took seats side by side. "Let me get Leah something to drink before we go through my homemade dessert options."

"Dessert options?" Joseph asked. "I don't

remember the last time I had homemade dessert, other than at one of the local bakeries. I'm sure anything will be wonderful."

"*Ach,* well . . . I hope you aren't disappointed." Sadie turned to Leah. "Would you like some milk?"

Leah nodded, and after she'd poured milk into a plastic glass, she asked Joseph if he would like coffee, and he nodded. "*Ya,* great."

Sadie placed the glass of milk in front of Leah, who immediately picked it up, took a sip, and then the glass slipped from her hands, hitting the table before it landed on the floor and rolled across the room leaving a trail of milk in its wake.

Leah sprinted from the chair, crouched down on her knees, and covered her head with both hands as she whimpered.

Sadie moved quickly and knelt by Leah, ready to tell her that spilled milk was literally nothing to be so upset about. But Joseph was quickly on Leah's other side and trying to pull the girl into his arms. She fought him, thrashing her arms, and screaming so loud that Sadie stood, numbed by what she saw.

"Stop it, Leah!" Joseph yelled as he tried to constrain the girl in his arms. "What have I told you about this? No one is going to hurt you."

Sadie began to tremble all over. Those were the exact words her father used to tell her mother before he beat her.

Chapter 12

Joseph's expression was taut with strain as he gently scooped Leah into his arms. After she was settled in a chair, he sat beside her.

Sadie's knees were weak, but she slowly pulled out a chair and sat across from father and daughter with trembling hands.

Still sobbing, Leah lifted her eyes to Sadie. "I'm sorry! I'm sorry I spilled *mei* milk."

"Leah, there is no harm done." Sadie reached over to touch Leah's hand, but the girl pulled it away. "I have a milking cow in the barn, so I never have a shortage of milk. You needn't cry, sweet *maedel.*" She turned to Joseph and glared at him, and she was tempted to tell him to leave right away and never come back. But then she couldn't keep an eye on Leah.

"Sorry about that. I thought we were past all that." Joseph said, not making eye contact with Sadie from where she sat across from him and Leah. Instead, he put an arm around his daughter, kissed her on the forehead, and said, "You're okay, Leah."

I thought we were past all that. Sadie wasn't sure a person ever completely recovered from abuse, but Leah was young. Maybe she would get through this without the bitterness Sadie had carried in her heart.

The child leaned into her father's embrace, and Sadie seethed on the inside. How many times had she seen her mother behave in the same way, usually following a good smack across the face? Her father always apologized, then took Sadie's mother into his arms as if it was perfectly normal to punch his wife, say he was sorry, and continue with the day. It had become the norm for Sadie's mother. She was not going to let it become the norm for Leah at such a young age.

"I-I think we need to go over the list of projects that I have around the *haus.*" She cleared her throat. "Before it gets too late."

It wasn't late at all, and Sadie was aware that she'd bypassed the dessert options, but she wanted Joseph to leave so she could think. Sadie would have done anything to ask him if Leah could spend the night, but she suspected Joseph wouldn't allow it. He had probably grilled the girl and made her promise not to tell what went on behind closed doors. Or was Sadie jumping to conclusions, her mind spooling with misconceptions?

She stood, reached for the list she'd made on the counter, then placed it on the table before quickly swiping up the mess on the floor. She poured Leah a fresh glass of milk. When the child didn't touch the glass and kept her head down, Sadie said, "I know you're thirsty, Leah." She smiled. "Remember, no crying over spilled milk. Go ahead and drink some."

Leah glanced at her father, who nodded, then she took the glass in both hands and took it to her mouth, gulping down several swigs before carefully setting it back on the table.

Sadie sat and nodded at the list. "As you can see . . ." She fought the shakiness in her voice, glancing at Leah, who now had her head against her father's shoulder again while Joseph took the paper in his hands. "I have listed fence repairs as the first item, and the most important, since I have a small herd of cows in that area." She paused and took a cleansing breath. "The water pump isn't working in the barn. I currently have a water hose I use from the outside faucet of the house to get water into their troughs." She chewed her lip as he continued to read.

"And I'm missing quite a few shingles from the last storm that blew through here."

She waited while he studied the list, but the vision of Leah crouched on the floor with her head covered wouldn't go away, and it was hard not to voice her newfound opinion of Joseph.

"These are all doable." Joseph handed her the paper. "I can start tomorrow if that suits you."

Nothing about Joseph Yoder suited Sadie, but she was going to have to agree so she could keep an eye on Leah. She'd have the girl in class, but this arrangement would give her extra time with Leah.

Sadie cleared her throat. "I wrote down a number at the bottom of the page. I know it's not the best hourly rate, but it's all I can afford, and —"

"It's fine," Joseph said before she could finish speaking.

Sadie racked her brain. *How can I spend more time with them?* Joseph would make a mistake in front of Sadie eventually, more than just yelling at his daughter. She had an idea.

"I'd like to prepare supper for you and Leah each day. I can bring Leah home with me from school, she'd have some play time while you finish working, then we could share a meal together." That was Sadie's best hope to spend as much time as she could with Joseph and his daughter. After she had enough proof that Joseph was causing harm to his daughter, she would go to the bishop. But she also had to consider that this was a behavior exhibited in the past, and perhaps Joseph was no longer a threat to his daughter. But in Sadie's experience, that type of violent behavior didn't just go away, at least not without counseling from the bishop or elders, something her mother wouldn't hear of, citing the embarrassment of it all. Leah was too young to make decisions in that regard, so Sadie would need to be her advocate.

Joseph pulled Leah a little closer to him as the girl buried her head in the nook of his shoulder. "The rate is fine. You don't need to prepare meals for us too."

Sadie couldn't read his stilled and stoic expression, so she opted for something to break the awkwardness clouding the room. She stood, went to the counter, and returned with two pies. "I almost forgot about dessert." She paused, forcing a smile. "Leah, I have pecan pie and rhubarb pie. Would you like a slice?"

Leah didn't look at her only shrugged.

"*Mei maedel,* you *lieb* pecan pie. Why

don't you have some?" Joseph gently nudged his daughter.

Sadie couldn't look at Joseph, but she was glad when Leah finally eased away from him and nodded.

Sadie lifted a slice of pecan pie onto a small plate already on the table and set it in front of her with a fork. "I hope you like it," she said, trying to sound cheerful.

"What do you tell Sadie?" Joseph said in a soft voice to his daughter.

"Danki." Leah forked a chunk of pie and slowly put it in her mouth, leaving Sadie no choice but to offer Joseph some pie.

He shook his head. "*Nee,* I'm afraid I'm fuller than I thought."

"I'm full also," Sadie said without looking at Joseph. She fought the urge to glare at the man sitting across the table from her, who only moments earlier were all for homemade desserts.

They sat in silence while Leah ate her pie. Occasionally, she glanced back and forth between Sadie and her father.

When Leah was done, it was hard for Sadie to send Leah home with Joseph when he said he was ready to go. But tomorrow, on the way home from school, Sadie planned to have a subtle talk with Leah.

The girl might open up without her father present.

Joseph wanted to tread lightly with Leah, who hadn't said much on the way home from Sadie's house. Now, as he tucked her into bed, he'd gotten the words straight in his mind and sorted out what he wanted to say. At least, he hoped so.

"*Mei* sweet butterfly . . ." He gently cupped her cheek as he gazed into her big brown eyes. "No one is ever going to hurt you again. I promised you that, right?"

She nodded, frowning, and Joseph wasn't sure if she would ever believe him. Time would have to be the prevailing proof that his word meant something. But, until then, Joseph would need to control his emotions when Leah reacted the way she did this evening. Scolding her was not going to help, but Joseph's recollections of certain situations outraged him and usually manifested as anger. Anger at himself.

"Sleep *gut, mei maedel,*" he said as he extinguished the flame on her lantern, then left the room.

After he made himself a cup of hot tea, he sat on the couch, dunking the teabag repeatedly until he sloshed tea over the side of his cup and into his lap. Tempted to curse, he took in a deep breath and decided prayer was a much better option. He knew the Lord had been testing his faith but now was not the time to abandon the only thing he'd always been able to count on.

He placed the tea on the coffee table, lowered his head into his hands, and for the first time in a long time, he wept. He cried for what used to be between him and Grace. He wept for the harm his daughter had endured. Grace was a woman with good qualities, but her temper and actions once she became a mother led to unforgivable memories, and Joseph had to put distance between them for the sake of his daughter.

He wept because he knew he couldn't keep running, hiding, and disregarding his responsibilities — to his daughter and to God.

Joseph needed help.

After taking a deep breath, he prayed aloud.

Dear *Gott,*

You have always been at the center of all my best intentions — to be a *gut* man, a *gut* husband, and a *gut* father. I strive to be a righteous man who lives a life that pleases You. But I have failed *mei* daughter, You, and myself. Please help me, Lord.

Then he wept again . . . mostly for Leah.

Chapter 13

Sadie loved her job. Most of the time. But today, she'd been on edge and felt anxious about several aspects of her life.

Henry was clearly avoiding her. Normally, she would see him several times throughout the day — when the children were at recess, or he'd pop in to say hello during lunch, and sometimes, he would wave from outside the window where he would be watering plants or mowing. Today, he might as well have been invisible.

When it was time to leave, she was also anxious to talk to Leah, but she knew better than to push the child too hard. She wasn't a psychologist, but she liked to think that she had a good understanding of children in general, after all her years of teaching. And about children in peril, in one way or another. There were times when Sadie's father had hit her mother so hard that Sadie swore she could physically feel it herself, which was impossible, but at the time, the inflicted emotional pain blurred with the physical pain her mother went through.

"Are you ready to go, Leah?" Sadie moved slowly to where Leah was still seated at her desk. The room had cleared out, and all the children had been picked up or walked home. "You remember that your *daed* is working at *mei haus, ya*? I'm going to take you home with me."

"Was it bad of me to give you those flowers?" Leah nodded to the roses on Sadie's desk. "I know *Daed* probably told you that I cut them from our bush and brought them to you."

Sadie knelt so she was at eye level with Leah. "*Nee,* it was not bad of you at all. They are lovely, and I probably forgot to say *danki.* It was a very nice thing to do."

After Sadie stood, Leah got out of her seat and grabbed her small backpack and lunchpail. "I was thinking that you might like *mei daed* and become *mei mudder.*"

Sadie swallowed hard as she motioned Leah to walk with her out of the school building. After she locked the door and they started toward her buggy, Sadie said, "I do like your *daed.*" She cleared her throat, unsure how she felt about Joseph. "And you have a *mudder* already." When Leah didn't say anything, Sadie said, "But I'd be very happy to be a *gut* friend to you if you'd like that."

Leah nodded as they got into the buggy.

Sadie pulled back on the reins and began to back up the horse, then guided the buggy onto the two-lane road. "And you know what that means, *ya*? Friends can trust one another and share if something bad is happening."

Leah remained quiet, her eyes fixated on the road in front of them.

"I saw you talking with Miriam today at recess," Sadie said. Miriam was another child that Sadie worried about a lot. Lloyd's daughter didn't show her emotions as much as her father, but the child's grief must be immeasurable, having lost her mother at such a young age.

"Her mother died," Leah said with little emotion, keeping her eyes focused on the road ahead.

Sadie nodded, trying to buy herself some time as she kept the horse at a slow trot. "*Ya,* she did. I think she misses her a lot." She paused, but Leah didn't acknowledge the comment. "I'm sure you miss your *mudder* too." Sadie glanced at Leah.

There it was. Out in the open. But no comment from the little girl.

Sadie didn't want to lose her balance on this fine line, but she needed something from Leah, any hint at what was going on in her life. "Leah, do you know where your *mudder* is now?" She cleared her throat. "Is she still in Pennsylvania?"

Leah finally turned to Sadie, her bottom lip trembling. "I'm not supposed to talk about it."

Sadie subtly released the breath she'd been holding. "Okay. But I'm happy to listen if you want to talk to someone."

"Miriam said that you talked to her when her *mudder* died and that you made her feel better." Leah raised one of her small eyebrows. "All the *kinner* say you're the nicest person they know."

Sadie's heart was momentarily full. "I'm glad that *mei* talk with Miriam made her feel better. It's difficult to lose someone we *lieb,* but we also must realize that they are in heaven and enjoying paradise with Jesus." She smiled, recalling her chat with Miriam right after her mother had passed. "And I'm glad the *kinner* think I'm a nice person. I *lieb* being a teacher."

"But *mei mudder* isn't dead." Leah cringed, then turned her gaze back toward the road in front of them.

Sadie needed to tread even more carefully,

but if she wasn't overt, she wasn't going to get any answers. "*Ya,* I know. I heard your *daed* say that she left. Do you know where she is?" She held her breath, then silently prayed that she wouldn't cross that invisible line that somehow connected them.

"Nee."

Sadie stayed quiet as she wondered what kind of mother would leave her child if she knew her husband was abusive. Maybe she was wrong. Perhaps Leah had behavioral issues, and Joseph had merely reacted out of frustration.

As a child, Sadie was aware of the abuse that was ongoing in her household, but her mother had protected Sadie, going as far as to bury money that Sadie would later use to buy her home.

When they pulled into Sadie's driveway, Joseph was working on the fence. If Leah wouldn't provide any answers, maybe Joseph would. However, her suspicions about him had surely shown through and seemingly created distance between them. But she felt an overwhelming desire to protect this little girl.

After she told Leah to go inside and help herself to any of the snacks Sadie had left out on the table, she marched to where Joseph was working on the fence. By the time she reached him, he had walked away, laid down his hammer and nails in the grass, and was squatting in front of a calf, the mother nearby and wailing.

"What's wrong?" she asked as she neared him, flinching at the painful cries coming from the small animal. The calf was only a few months old and voicing his objection to whatever Joseph was doing as the mother's yowling increased.

Sadie lowered herself down beside Joseph, then gasped at what she saw.

"There must have been some loose barbed wire somewhere in the pasture, and her back leg is tangled in it." He glanced at Sadie with an urgency in his eyes. "Go get some towels soaked with warm water, and if you have any anti-infection medication, grab that too. And some gauze. I need to finish getting this untangled."

Sadie took out the handkerchief she always had in the pocket of her apron and pressed it against the spot Joseph had freed on the calf's front leg. "Use this for now." Then she got up and ran to the house, rushing around to get supplies.

"What's wrong?" Leah asked from her seat at the kitchen table, with a mouthful of cookie.

"A calf is injured, and I need to get some

medicine and bandages to your *daed.*"

Sadie rushed to the bathroom and gathered gauze, tape, and a small pair of scissors from her bathroom medicine cabinet, along with a tube of antibacterial gel.

Leah stood like she was going to follow Sadie. She still chewed on a cookie as she walked barefoot across the living room.

"I think you should stay here," Sadie said as she recalled the blood on the calf and the wailing from the mother.

Leah stopped in her tracks, swallowed, then said, "Don't worry, Sadie. *Daed* is *gut* at doctoring boo-boos."

Sadie could hear the animals wailing, and she knew Joseph needed the supplies in her hands, but her chest tightened. She'd noticed the scar on Leah's left lower arm the first day she'd shown up in school. *Now or never.* "Did he doctor your arm, where the scar is?"

Leah nodded as she smiled. "*Ya,* he did."

Sadie wanted to ask her how it happened, but more yowling from the cows told her now wasn't the time.

By the time she reached Joseph and got on her knees beside him, he had freed the calf from the barbed wire and was holding her handkerchief against the spot that had been bleeding the most.

"She's going to be okay." He petted the calf's head with his free hand. "We will get you all fixed up," he said in a gentle voice to the animal before he began doctoring the wound and wrapping the spot in gauze.

After he was done, he said, "Momma isn't going to like it . . ." He glanced at the huge cow only a few feet away with her mouth open and continuing to make an awful sound. ". . . but we need to keep this little girl separate from the rest of the herd so she can heal." He looked at Sadie, his eyes kind and sympathetic, but with a sense of urgency.

Sadie glanced at the calf's mother, and it was impossible not to make the connection to Leah being ripped away from her mother. Even though Joseph and Leah had said Grace left them, Sadie suspected that wasn't the truth.

"But that cow is still nursing, and if we keep the baby away from the mother, she might not let her continue to feed," she said as Joseph leaned down and carefully lifted the calf into his arms.

"Is there a stall in the barn large enough for the mother and her calf?"

"Ya." Sadie nodded toward the barn and stood.

As they left with Joseph carrying the calf,

Sadie followed.

She wasn't sure she'd ever witnessed such tenderness with an animal. Joseph continued to stroke the young calf's head as he spoke in a comforting voice. "You'll be all right. We'll be right back with your *mamm.*"

When he stood, he brushed hay from his black pants. "You're right. There's room for the mother." He reached for a harness hanging nearby. "Hopefully, she'll cooperate."

Sadie bent at the waist and stroked the calf's head, and only a few minutes later, Joseph returned, leading the animal with ease, and she seemed to know exactly where her calf was.

It took a few minutes for both to settle, and Joseph arranged feed and water nearby so Momma could reach it easily.

"I'll check the rest of the pasture to make sure there isn't anything else that could be harmful to your other animals."

"I don't know how that barbed wire got out there." Sadie scratched her cheek, feeling badly that this calf had found danger on her land. But she had a more pressing question burning her like a branding iron. "When will Leah be back with her *mudder*?" She folded her arms across her chest and raised her chin.

"What?" Joseph asked when he locked

eyes with Sadie's inquiring glare.

"You said she left. But why?"

Joseph lowered his head, kicked at the straw floor in the barn, then looked back up at Sadie. "I really don't want to talk about this."

I bet you don't. How many times had Sadie heard her father say, *"Everything is fine, and there's no need to speak of this."* It was always after he'd hurt her mother in some way. And Sadie and her mother never mentioned it. That was then, when Sadie was a child. She wasn't a kid anymore, but she could certainly be a friend to Leah.

Sadie opened her mouth, ready to demand answers, but she was distracted when a buggy pulled into the driveway. She exited the barn, Joseph on her heels.

Oh, no.

There couldn't have been a worse time for Lizzie and Esther to show up. The matchmakers of Montgomery, Indiana. Or maybe it was the best time for the elderly sisters to arrive. They could get a person to say just about anything, no matter how mysterious the man or woman might be.

"I'm not sure why Lizzie and Esther are here," she said as she kept her eyes on the buggy. Lizzie's husband usually drove the women around, and sure enough . . . she could see him in the front seat as the two elderly women slowly got out of the buggy. "But there is something you should know about these sisters." She glanced at Joseph, who held his hand to his forehead, blocking the sun as he watched the two women slowly making their way toward the barn. "They are notorious matchmakers. Everyone who lives here knows it. Just ignore anything that they might say." She glanced at Joseph, who frowned.

"Okay," he said as an even more somber expression crept across his face. Despite the circumstances — her suspicions about Joseph and her feelings about falling in love — it was disappointing that Joseph didn't welcome the idea of being fixed up with Sadie. Was it because he was married, or because he wasn't attracted to her at all? *Maybe both.* And why did it matter? She'd seen another side of Joseph Yoder.

"And whatever you do, please don't mention about the secret admirer note," she added before the two women were in earshot.

Chapter 14

Joseph knew it was only a matter of time before his untruths were revealed, but he planned to choose his words carefully. He just needed to make enough money so he and Leah could move on. He'd only rented the house they were in. Even though he'd hoped this could be a permanent and stable place for him and Leah, the community was too small to keep secrets, and his was going to get out soon.

The smaller of the two women walked toward Joseph and Sadie with long strides, her face crinkled, and with her eyes hidden behind a pair of dark shades. Her sister, a much larger woman, trailed behind with a slight limp, also donning black shades.

"You're Joseph Yoder. You're from Pennsylvania, and you are here with your daughter, Leah. I've seen you at worship service, but you always leave right after the meal." Lizzie lowered her shades on her nose and peered at Joseph above the rim as her eyebrows rose. "You have a beard, so you must be married. Where is your *fraa*?"

"Lizzie," her sister said breathlessly as she sidled up to her. "Have you ever even introduced yourself to this man?"

"Nee." Lizzie kept her eyes on Joseph. "As I said, he and his daughter leave immediately after we eat on Sundays." She paused, lifted her chin, still focused on Joseph. "Almost like you're sneaking out and avoiding folks."

"Lizzie!" Her sister snapped harder this time before she turned to Joseph. "Please forgive *mei* sister, Lizzie. She can be a little brazen for some people." The older woman extended her hand. "I am Esther." It was a gentle exchange, despite the woman's large hand. "Lizzie and I own The Peony Inn." She smiled. "Lizzie's husband is in the buggy and sends his apologies for not getting out. He has a sprained ankle."

Were they waiting for him to answer the question about his wife? "I'm Joseph." He glanced at the little woman — Lizzie. "But you already know that." He cut his eyes to where Sadie was standing to his left. She chewed on her bottom lip as she kept her eyes down. Joseph was sure that his loss of temper the day before had been a surprise to Sadie. He was disappointed with himself for not handling the situation better.

"So, where is your *fraa*?" Lizzie spoke louder this time.

Esther groaned. "Stop badgering this man."

Lizzie's expression softened. "She's right. I'm sorry. You must be a widower since your *fraa* isn't here."

Esther stomped a foot. "Be quiet, Lizzie."

When Joseph was in his running-around years, he'd gone to the movies and recalled the characters referencing 'good cop/bad cop'. This was like watching the same thing.

Sadie cleared her throat and offered up a weak smile. "Joseph is doing some work for me." She nodded toward the fence where one post was leaning. "And he just finished untangling a calf that had gotten into some barbed wire."

Joseph appreciated her interjection, but Lizzie was still staring a hole through him and waiting for an answer. Sighing, he looped his thumbs through his suspenders, then locked eyes with the small woman. He'd be leaving soon anyway, after he'd saved enough money to move on. Past experiences had proven that secrets could be blown radically out of proportion. In this moment, he decided to voice his partial version of the truth, then ask God to forgive him later.

"*Mei fraa* is alive." He paused. "I'm sad to say that Grace, *mei fraa,* chose to go live in the *Englisch* world. *Mei* daughter, Leah, and I came here for a fresh start." He took a deep breath and hoped his response would be enough to satisfy Lizzie.

Esther gasped. "I know of a couple this happened to." She glanced at her sister, who nodded. "The woman sought out an *Englisch* divorce."

Lizzie took off her shades. "Is that what happened to you? Your *fraa* ran off and left you for another man? Did she divorce you? If so, the bishop knows you have no control over such things, and maybe you can remarry." She smiled broadly as she turned to Sadie.

Joseph wished it were that simple. Sadie seemed like the type of woman who he could fall in love with, if he ever thought he could trust another woman again. She also seemed to love children. "That's exactly what happened." The sting of the lie bore into him like a nail in his heart even though a partial truth was buried beneath the surface.

Lizzie stepped closer and had just opened her mouth to speak when the screen door slammed, and Leah came onto the porch. The sisters turned around, both smiling.

"She's a darling *maedel,*" Esther said. "We spent time with her at the library recently."

Joseph nodded as he recalled he and Leah going to the library. Joseph had checked out a book on raising a child as a single parent. His daughter had spent time in the children's section.

"Please don't speak of this in front of her," Joseph said quickly. He'd instructed Leah not to talk to anyone about their situation, but these women might drag the truth out of her. Hopefully, that hadn't already happened at the library.

Lizzie patted Joseph's arm. "Don't you worry about a thing, young man. We are nothing if not discreet."

Joseph glanced at Sadie who cast her gaze down, shaking her head slightly.

Lizzie pointed a finger at Sadie, waiting for her to look up. "You know that to be true." Then she smiled and winked at Sadie before turning to Leah, who was crossing the front yard and heading toward them.

Joseph had dodged a bullet — another term he'd picked up at the movies.

The women began a conversation with Leah, and they didn't mention anything about Grace. Joseph sensed that discreet probably wasn't a word associated with these ladies, but he was glad they were talking about cookies, school, and other generic subjects.

After a few minutes chatting with Leah, the women excused themselves and strolled back to their buggy where Lizzie's husband had stayed behind.

"Tell Ben I hope he feels better," Sadie said as she waved.

The women nodded, then Lizzie looked over her shoulder and winked at Sadie.

Sadie was sure that Lizzie and Esther's only reason for stopping by was to confirm Joseph's English divorce. But Joseph had told Sadie that he was married and never mentioned a divorce. Maybe he just didn't want to be on her list of suspects. The truth about Joseph was likely tied up somewhere in the middle like a knot that would never be loose. Either way, she and Joseph were now on their matchmaking radar, a place Sadie didn't want to be — with anyone — especially Joseph.

She asked Leah if she would like to collect eggs for her since she'd forgotten this morning. The child nodded enthusiastically before she skipped to the barn.

When Leah was out of sight, she turned

to Joseph, more confused than ever. She replayed the conversation between him and Lizzie and Esther in her mind. Was Grace a terrible person who chose another man over her child? Especially if her husband was harming their child? Or was she completely wrong about Joseph? Leah could have been acting out because of the separation between her parents.

"I am sorry that your *fraa* left you for another man." She sighed. "That must be awful." Sadie could understand why Joseph would want a fresh start. "But you should probably know, that since you said you are divorced, legally, you are now on Lizzie and Esther's radar. Even though it isn't allowed for our people to remarry unless a spouse dies, they will try to find a loophole." She shook her head. After she rolled her eyes, she said, "I've been on their radar for a long time, but this new information is going to have them trying to play matchmaker between the two of us."

"I'm not in the market for *lieb.*" He grinned. "Besides, someone is already pursuing you."

Sadie flinched, frowning. "Pursuing, in a creepy way." She smiled at him. "And while I appreciate you not mentioning the secret admirer letter, the sisters will still try to play matchmaker for you and me."

Joseph stroked the length of his beard. "How did they already know so much about me?"

Sadie shrugged. "I'm sure that when you came into town, they made a mad rush to inquire where you came from and what you and your daughter were doing here. They probably picked up bits and pieces here and there."

"*Ya,* I guess. I'm sure I've mentioned that we came from Pennsylvania, and of course some of the men know *mei* name. I've probably even met Lizzie's husband while dining with the men after church services."

Leah emerged from the barn, her hands holding her black apron curled in front of her. "Twelve eggs!" she said proudly.

"Wonderful." Sadie pressed her palms together. "*Danki* for doing that, Leah. There's a bowl on the counter if you'd like to carry them inside for me."

Leah glanced back and forth between Sadie and Joseph as she smiled, then nodded.

Sadie weighed out her thoughts and considered, again, whether she might have misread Joseph, largely influenced by her own childhood with her father. This new information meant he might be technically available, depending on the bishop's stance. But he'd said he wasn't in the market for love. Understandable. And Sadie wasn't either.

"Well, we will have to tolerate Lizzie and Esther's antics, but since neither of us is seeking a relationship, they will lose interest in us." She chuckled, which felt good. "Eventually."

Joseph grinned, and Sadie briefly wondered if she would change her mind about love if Joseph did. She wondered if part of Joseph's allure was the mysterious air about him. Because, no matter what he said . . . Sadie was sure he wasn't telling the entire truth. In the back of her mind, she couldn't shake the feeling that maybe he had hurt Leah at some point, but she needed proof.

"I'm going to start supper," she said, looking forward to not eating alone again. "Meatloaf, so it won't take too long."

Joseph pointed to the barn. "I'll check on the calf and mother, then wash up."

Sadie nodded, then watched him walk away. For a few moments, she pictured herself romantically involved with Joseph, but just as quickly, she saw her father's face and knew she couldn't trust Joseph. *Not yet anyway.* There were some gray areas that needed investigating. And she had her own investigation going related to her mysterious note.

As she slowly made her way to the house, she thought about her list. After seeing Henry with the woman — Gretchen — she felt like she could rule him out as the author of the note. She was certain it wasn't Joseph. So, that left Lloyd and Paul. At first, she'd thought Lloyd was in too much grief to consider courtship. But he admitted that he needed a wife, so he was still on her list. Paul remained a contender, and he had even shown a softer side of himself. Maybe Montgomery's playboy was thinking about settling down.

Or was Sadie completely wrong in her way of thinking? Was there another mystery man out there vying for her affection?

"Hmm . . ." she said softly as she walked up the porch steps.

Chapter 15

Lloyd set a plate in front of Miriam. "The scrambled eggs are runny, and the toast is burnt a little, but it's better than *mei* last attempt." He kissed his daughter on the forehead. "But you won't have to endure *mei* terrible cooking for much longer."

Miriam slathered butter on her toast. "What will we do, go out to eat?"

There was a hint of joy in her voice, which was nice, but going to restaurants wasn't feasible daily. "Sometimes we will go out, but I've come up with a solution and found someone to help us."

Miriam was quiet as she set her toast down and began to move the runny eggs around on her plate. "Like a new *mamm*?"

Lloyd's chest tightened. He could never replace Annie, but he had to put his daughter's best interest ahead of his own. "I guess you could say that." A woman in the house would teach Miriam how to cook, make sure her dress wasn't on inside out, prepare meals, assure that she didn't forget her lunch . . . and all the other things Lloyd was failing at.

"When will she be here?" Miriam asked with a sunny cheerfulness that he'd missed.

Lloyd carried a plate for himself to the table and sat across from his daughter. "Soon," he said, trying to sound upbeat and hoping Miriam wouldn't ask any more questions that he didn't have the answers for.

Only a few minutes later, he was glad when she finished everything on her plate. *"Danki, Daed,"* she said as she carried her plate to the sink.

"And I made your lunch last night. It's in the refrigerator."

Miriam retrieved her lunch and set it on the table, then she smiled. "I miss *Mamm,* but I'm glad you won't have to do all this *fraa* stuff anymore."

That was her sweet way of telling him that she was going to be glad to have organization and good meals again. "I'm not very *gut* at it," he said with a shrug.

"You shouldn't have to be. It's work for girls." She picked up her lunch before she glanced at the clock on the wall.

Lloyd stood, still eating his toast, and he

had to admit that while his solution wasn't perfect, it was the best he could come up with.

After Paul dropped his nephew off at school the next day, he recalled his conversation with Sadie again.

"Paul, it is inappropriate for you to have your nephew relay a message from you — that you think I'm pretty — and it's even more unacceptable for you to send a note with him to leave on mei *desk. Please don't pursue me in a romantic way."*

Her words still stung. She'd shot down his attempts to court her in the past, and clearly her opinion of him hadn't changed. He had to admit that he'd only made things worse by telling Adam to tell her he thought she was pretty, but he hadn't lost hope that she might let him into her heart, if only a little. He was tired of spending time with women outside of their community. It went against everything he'd been brought up to know as good and righteous.

He shook his head as he picked up speed in his buggy. *I'm going to make some changes.* Paul wanted to be a better man. Maybe his attempts to show confidence had come across as arrogance instead.

As his thoughts scampered about, one

thing was for sure . . . he needed to adjust his attitude when it came to women and be more respectful. He doubted he would ever have a chance with Sadie Miller, but maybe there was a woman out there who could see inside Paul's soul and understand the man he wanted to be.

After sorting through his thoughts, he recalled Sadie's mention of a note — a secret admirer, she'd said. He ran names in his mind. Who could have done such a thing? It must be a fellow who was single or widowed.

It wasn't Lloyd. The man was too filled with grief over the recent loss of his wife. And it wasn't Henry. During one of Paul's outings into the English world, he'd caught Henry in a local tavern with a woman, and it was obvious that they were more than friends. Even in Paul's eyes, their behavior had been inappropriate and crossed too many lines. They'd been openly affectionate in public, hugging and kissing.

And that only left one other person that Paul could think of. Joseph Yoder. He was new to town, kept to himself, and avoided conversation. Paul had tried to talk to him after worship service a couple of times, and the man answered with one-word responses. The most Paul had gotten out of Joseph was that he was from Pennsylvania. He had a beard, so he was married or widowed. Whatever his story, he kept it close to his chest and had even walked away when Joseph had asked him about his marital status.

He had to be the one — Sadie's secret admirer. There wasn't anyone else.

Paul shrugged it off. He had his own problems. If he was going to find a wife, someone to help him raise Adam, he needed to change. That was going to be his focus. Hopefully, Joseph Yoder was a good man. Sadie deserved a good man. He'd always found it odd that she'd never married. Maybe she'd been waiting for the right man to come along. And it surely wasn't Paul.

He'd pray about it all — that he would be the man God meant him to be, and that Joseph would be a good fit for Sadie — if it was God's will.

After a few days of working for Sadie, it was apparent that Joseph's daughter liked Sadie a lot. After school, they'd sit on swings in the yard, and it was music to Joseph's ears when they laughed. Leah hadn't shown much joy since they'd left Pennsylvania, and it warmed his heart that she'd found comfort in Sadie's company. Despite his desire to lay down roots in Montgomery, Joseph and Leah would most likely have to leave at some point. Grace would find them. Somehow, she always did. His former wife would flash her legal English divorce documents showing that she had custody of Leah and try to take their daughter from him. Joseph was never going to let that happen.

He cringed at the thought of leaving, especially since Leah seemed to be getting attached to Sadie, which was surprising. Sadie had slowly chipped away at the armor his daughter had constructed when it came to trusting women. For the hundredth time, Joseph wondered why Sadie had never married. She'd made it clear that a romantic union didn't interest her.

Joseph had pondered it, mostly late at night when her face came into his mind's eye, the way her cheeks dimpled when she smiled and her emerald, green eyes twinkled. She was a beautiful woman, and Joseph wished more than anything that their situations were different. Mostly, he loved the way that Sadie was with Leah.

It concerned him that they still didn't know who Sadie's secret admirer was, although Joseph was pretty sure he had a viable guess. Sadie remained rather aloof around Joseph, but she'd shared with him that Henry was staying out of sight for the most part. She said she found that unusual. Perhaps he was embarrassed about getting caught with the English woman.

Whatever the reason, Joseph had a strong hunch that Henry wrote the anonymous letter, and it left him with a weird feeling in his gut. *Jealousy? Or fear for Sadie?*

Henry pulled up his trousers, affixed his suspenders over his blue shirt, then looked over at Gretchen still in the bed, her long blonde hair sweeping across the white comforter like angel wings. But there was nothing angelic about what they were doing, and Henry felt even worse since they'd met at a seedy motel just outside of town.

"I'm not going to be staying in town much longer." Gretchen stretched her arms high as she yawned. It was slightly after four in the afternoon, when Henry got off work, but his new friend kept odd sleeping hours, sometimes starting her day at two in the morning. He glanced at the bottles of pills on the nightstand. She said she took them to sleep, but the woman didn't seem to sleep much at all, and the medication caused her eyes to become glassy. Sometimes, she slurred her speech.

"Why won't you be staying in town?" he asked as he turned back around, then slipped into his black leather shoes. It was a double-edged sword for sure. Henry couldn't seem to reject her advances. If she was gone, the temptation would move along with her.

"It's just time for me to go."

He glanced over his shoulder just in time to see her sit up. The covers slipped to her waist, revealing her naked upper half, fueling the guilt that had settled in the pit of Henry's stomach. He turned away from her.

Henry had no idea what Gretchen's story was, where she worked, or where she was from. He wasn't sure he wanted to know. If he didn't know where to find her after she left, he wouldn't be tempted to get in touch with her.

"I'm sorry to hear that," he lied. "I've enjoyed our time together." It was true. He liked being with her, but the guilt afterward wasn't worth it.

"Where are you going?" he asked anyway.

"Home."

Don't ask, don't ask.

Gretchen didn't wear a wedding ring, but that didn't necessarily mean she wasn't married or didn't have a significant other wherever home was. That would add another layer of guilt.

He cleared his throat. "When are you leaving?"

She sighed before she reached for the bottle of pills on the nightstand, popping at least one into her mouth, followed by a small drink of water. "Not sure. But soon."

Henry squeezed his eyes shut, willing himself not to look at her. But when he did, she patted the bed where he'd been. "One last time?" She batted her glassy eyes at him.

He took in the entirety of her slender body laid out on the bed, then slipped out of his shoes, dropped his suspenders, and climbed in beside her, knowing he would not feel good about himself later.

Chapter 16

Sadie spread the red and white checkered blanket on the ground. A full sun shone, and the breeze was just cool enough to make for a perfect spring day by the creek. This was the first time she'd spent a Saturday with Joseph and Leah . . . and they had an extra person today.

She set the picnic basket down, packed for four people. "I'm glad Miriam wanted to come spend the day with Leah." She sat across from Joseph on the blanket while the girls waded at the edge of the shallow creek.

Joseph had continued to work for Sadie over the past two weeks, and not once had she seen another episode between him and Leah. He was kind to his daughter, to Sadie, and he even arrived early each morning to check on the animals. The injured calf and mother had been returned to the herd after four days and were thriving as if nothing had happened.

After seeing to the critters, he would begin checking off items on Sadie's list — a list that was growing shorter and would be completed soon. They had supper each evening, the conversations often including laughter, and a week ago, they had started sharing devotions after the meal.

Joseph sat when Sadie did. "I'm glad too. They each suffered the loss of their *mudders.*" He paused. "In the beginning, that's what drew them together as friends, but listen . . ." He cupped one ear and put a finger to his lips.

Sadie looked at the girls and smiled. "There's nothing like the sound of *kinner's* laughter." When she turned back to Joseph, he was staring at her in a way she'd caught him doing often lately. "What?" she asked.

"I just don't get it." He shook his head. "Why aren't you married and raising a family of your own?"

They had mostly avoided relationship subjects since they'd first met, and even more so since Esther and Lizzie's visit, but here it was out in the open now. Sadie had never told anyone her secret. "I-I just don't really trust men."

Joseph tipped his head to one side, then stroked his beard. She waited for him to ask why, but he stayed quiet. This might be a path into his past.

"I'm sure you don't trust women, either, after your *fraa* left you." *Would he share more?* Sadie had always sensed that there was more. She'd almost abandoned all thoughts about him abusing Leah. It seemed to Sadie that she would have seen some sort of sign by now. They'd spent plenty of time together.

"I trust *you,*" he said softly, his eyes locked with hers.

She wasn't expecting his response and quickly looked away.

"But you don't trust me." The sadness in Joseph's voice indicated this bothered him.

"I-I do now," she said after a while, glad he hadn't questioned her as to why she didn't trust men in general.

"I guess I was kind of aloof in the beginning." He stretched his legs and crossed one ankle over the other as he leaned back on his hands.

When he didn't elaborate, Sadie began to unpack the picnic basket. "And now? You said you trust me . . ." She locked eyes with him again. "I don't want to pry though."

But I really want to know your story.

Joseph liked Sadie a lot, as much as he'd liked his wife before he fell in love with her.

But he knew how quickly things could change. People weren't always who they seemed to be. He'd meant it when he said he trusted her, as much as he was capable. Joseph had been around her long enough that he wanted to believe she was genuine.

"*Mei fraa,* Grace, she wasn't cut out for married life." He paused, hesitant to go on. "And — and she wasn't doing a great job being a *mudder.*" It was the most he'd ever told anyone, except for the bishop and elders back home. And they hadn't believed him. *What if Sadie doesn't believe me?*

"I would think that being a parent is a hard job." She smiled. "Although, having been around *kinner* so much, I believe it must be very rewarding also."

Joseph wanted to hear Sadie's story, why she didn't trust men. He would have to share his. Sighing, he said, "Grace was . . ." He held his breath before he released it and went on. "She was physical with Leah. I mean, she would hit her when she misbehaved. Not spankings. She would strike her across the face, and one time she threw her against a wall so hard that it knocked her out." He blinked his eyes to keep tears from forming as he recalled that day. "I knew I needed to do something, to protect Leah, so I went to the bishop and the elders." He lifted his eyes to Sadie's. Her jaw hung open, and she had tears in her eyes.

"What happened in the kitchen with the spilled milk," he went on, "was *mei* frustration with myself for not getting Leah away from Grace sooner. Her outbursts have mostly stopped and so have her nightmares." He tried to smile. "Since we've been spending time with you." He paused, meeting Sadie's teary gaze. "I wasn't sure she'd ever trust another woman again."

Sadie covered her face with her hands. *"Ach, nee,"* she said through tears as she shook her head.

Joseph glanced at the girls, who were still playing at the edge of the creek, before he inched his way closer to Sadie, putting a hand on her arm. "Please don't cry." He wasn't sure why the sudden onslaught of tears, unless it was just the subject matter that was so upsetting.

She dropped her hands to her lap. "You don't understand. I thought it was you! I've seen the kind of fear that Leah displayed that day in the kitchen, then when you reacted the way you did, I assumed that you were abusing her." She took a handkerchief from her apron pocket and dabbed at her eyes. "I'm so sorry."

Joseph frowned with confusion. "What

made you decide to trust me after thinking that?"

"No one with that instinct to be so angry can be around someone without showing his or her true colors. You've been nothing but kind to me and to Leah." She shrugged, sniffling. "I decided I had been wrong, but how does a *mudder* do such a thing as Grace, and . . ." She gasped. "I automatically assumed that Leah was showing fear because of you." She shook her head. "Again, I'm sorry. That was so wrong of me, but *mei daed* . . ." She stopped and pinched her lips closed for a few moments. "He . . . he . . ."

Joseph touched her arm. "Did your *daed* hurt you as a child?"

She quickly shook her head. "*Nee.* Never."

Joseph rubbed her arm. "Then . . ." He didn't understand.

"I've never told anyone this." She sniffled. "He beat *mei mudder,* a lot. I assumed all men had that deep inside somewhere. I guess that's why it was so easy for me to recognize the fear and automatically think you were harming Leah."

Joseph pulled her into his arms. "I'm so sorry you had to go through that." He cupped the back of her head as she cried.

She swiped at her eyes before she eased

him away. "*Danki,* but you said Grace left you and Leah. Is that true?"

Joseph hung his head. "*Nee,* not all of it." The weight of his lies kept him from looking at her. "When I went to the bishop to tell him what was happening in our *haus,* he didn't believe me." He glanced up at Sadie. "The bishop is Grace's father, and he took her word over mine, insisting that I was the abusive parent. Grace told her father that what I'd done was unforgivable and that she couldn't live with me anymore. And, as you know, divorce is forbidden. I refused to be counseled because I knew the truth about Grace, and that her treatment of Leah was only getting worse. Grace chose to leave our way of life, got an English divorce, and retained custody of Grace. Her father shunned her after that, and maybe things would have been different if Leah had told the truth about her *mamm.* But she was scared and wouldn't talk about it." He paused as he recalled Grace taking Leah out of their home for the last time, pulling her much too hard by the arm as they left. "I should have done more to stop what was happening, but divorce isn't even something we believe in. I thought I would at least be able to see Leah and eventually make Grace's father see that his daughter was the one who wasn't able to parent his granddaughter without causing her harm." He paused as he swallowed with difficulty. "So here comes the hard part, full transparency, and you might not like me after hearing what I did."

Sadie didn't look like she was breathing. "Go on," she said barely above a whisper.

"Grace had enrolled Leah in an English school near where she lived. I didn't even get visitation rights. Looking back, I made so many mistakes and didn't understand what I was signing." He raised his shoulders, then relaxed them slowly as he shook his head. "I had no idea how a divorce works, and in *mei* mind, it wasn't relevant. Grace and I would be married for life, the way our people have always believed, and no piece of paper could change that in the eyes of *Gott.* But I didn't consider how the legal part of it would affect me seeing Leah — or not being able to see her. I missed her so much that it felt like a piece of me was gone. I was able to get Leah's attention one day while she was on the playground when the teacher was talking on her cell phone. I asked her if she wanted to come away with me." He paused as the memory threatened to take hold of him. "I noticed she had a bruise on her arm. She didn't hesitate. So, basically, I stole *mei* own daughter. We've been on the run since then."

Joseph knew he might have lost her now. He'd broken the rules of the *Ordnung* by lying and gone against God.

"I would have done the exact same thing." She spoke firmly, then threw her arms around him and hung on as if for dear life.

They stayed like that until they heard the rustling of grass from tiny feet approaching, then slowly eased away from each other.

"Look! Look!" Miriam bounced up on her toes. "Now you have a new *mudder* too!"

Joseph and Sadie looked at each other before Joseph asked Miriam, "You have a new *mamm*?"

Miriam nodded before she turned to Leah. "See! I told you that Sadie would be the best *mamm* ever! Now we both have *mudders*!"

Joseph held up a hand. "Hold on, *mei maeds.* Leah, Sadie is not your new *mudder.* We are *gut* friends." He smiled at Sadie, who had covered her mouth with her hand as if to keep from laughing.

Sadie lowered her hand and turned her attention to Miriam. "How could you have a new *mudder*? I've heard nothing about your *daed* courting anyone."

Miriam twirled a string from her prayer

covering with one finger. "She's almost a *mudder.* She cooks and cleans, and packs lunches and even reads me bedtime stories, all the stuff that *mudders* do, except she has her own bedroom, and she's got gray hair."

Sadie pressed on, grinning. "What is her name?"

"Lydia!" Miriam said proudly. "*Daed* said we can still miss *mamm,* and that Lydia will never be *mei* real *mudder,* but she makes things easier for me and *Daed.* And *Daed* called her something, but I can't remember."

"Did your *daed* say she was a nanny?"

"*Ya!* That's it," Miriam said before she turned to Leah. "Now you are going to get a *mamm* too."

Joseph smiled, and when Sadie returned the smile, he couldn't help but feel hopeful for what the future might bring. Maybe he'd stay in Montgomery after all.

Sadie finally got the girls to calm down as she reeled in the conversations they'd had. "Here, now, time to eat." She handed each of them a plate with a chicken salad sandwich, apple slices, and a small thermos of juice. Then she laid out the same things for her and Joseph.

She waited until after the girls had eaten

and gone back to the creek before she said, "How are you going to explain to Leah that I am not her new *mudder*?" Grinning, she admitted silently that she liked the sound of it.

Joseph shrugged. "I'm not."

Sadie rolled her eyes. "I guess I better get ready for *mei* wedding."

He chuckled. "You never know."

Something about the way he said it caused butterflies to swirl in Sadie's stomach, a feeling she wasn't familiar with. Maybe they were both letting their guard down somewhat because any developing feelings they might have for each other were trapped in a place where they could never be together romantically.

"By the way, I meant to tell you that you can cross Paul off your list of secret admirer suspects."

"I kind of already did based on *mei* conversation with him a few weeks ago. But why do you bring it up?"

"I saw him with an Amish woman at the bakery. They looked cozy."

Sadie took a sip of her juice as she thought about the note she'd received. "So, Paul is out. All Lloyd ever wanted was help with Miriam. He is still grieving his *fraa,* so I don't think he can be the author either. And

I caught Henry with that woman, and I just don't think he has those kinds of feelings for me." She shuddered as she recalled the way he'd acted when she spoke to him at the school.

Joseph put a hand on his heart. "I wasn't lying." He cringed. "At least not about the note. I didn't write the secret admirer letter." He leaned over and kissed her on the cheek. "Although I'm wishing I had."

Sadie warmed from head to toe as she felt a blush rise from her neck to fill her cheeks. *But this has nowhere to go.*

"Wait a minute," she said as she lifted her eyebrows and sat taller. "I think I might know who wrote the note."

"Who?" Joseph asked as his expression mirrored hers.

"We will find out tomorrow at worship service. And I won't stop until I get the truth. But I do have a hunch."

Sadie wondered why she hadn't considered this scenario before.

Chapter 17

Sadie rushed into the Stoltzfus' barn, nearly late for worship service. She had to take a seat in the back as she strained to see Joseph seated with the other men on the other side. The bishop was a large man, seated with the elders in the congregation. Tractors, hay bales, animals, and various tools and equipment had all been relocated to accommodate the crowd of around sixty.

Sadie leaned to her left, then to her right until she had a semi-clear view and eventually located Joseph, smiling, as if he was waiting for her to find him. She'd gone to sleep the night before with visions of him on her mind, recalling the embraces and kiss on the cheek. She was caring less and less about who her secret admirer might be.

Normally, Sadie embraced the three-hour church service, especially when a family's home wasn't large enough to hold everyone and they worshipped in the barn with the sounds of nature outside, but today she fidgeted as thoughts swirled in her mind. Perhaps, she'd been all wrong about who left her the note. She'd overlooked the two women who were famous for such tactics.

"*Wie bischt,* Lizzie and Esther." Sadie saw Benjamin across the room with the other men, so Sadie would need to talk quickly and get to the point before Benjamin joined his wife or Lizzie headed to the kitchen to help with the meal.

"I know what you did." Sadie crossed her arms across her chest.

The two elderly women glanced at each other before looking back at Sadie. "What did we do?" Lizzie mirrored Sadie's stance by folding her arms across her chest. Esther frowned as she raised an eyebrow at Sadie.

"When Joseph came into town, a single man, you began your matchmaking tactics the way you have always done." Sadie waited, but the sisters just glanced at each other again before Esther spoke.

"Sadie, we have tried to match you up with so many men over the years, I must admit . . . we've given up."

Sadie chuckled as she pointed a finger first at Esther, then at Lizzie. "You two never give up. That's why you wrote the secret admirer letter and left it on the desk at school. Joseph is truly the only eligible bachelor if you disregard the other men in our community. You thought you would give us a nudge." She thought about how if she'd never received the letter, she might not have gotten to know Joseph. Under different circumstances, the sisters might have done a good thing, but they didn't have all the facts.

Lizzie gasped as she put a finger to her chin. "You received a secret admirer letter, and you never told us?"

Esther took a step closer to Sadie, then spoke in a whisper. "What did it say? When did you receive it? It had to be from Joseph. He's new to town. How long are you into your courtship?"

"Wait. Whoa." Sadie shook her head. Lizzie might be known to tell a tall tale now and then, but not Esther. "Can you really look me in the face and tell me that neither of you wrote the note?"

Lizzie bounced up on her toes. "*Ach,* this is so thrilling. Did Joseph confess to writing the letter? What did it say?" She glanced at Sadie's apron pockets. "Do you have it with you?"

Sadie's stomach lurched as she brought a hand to her chest. "You really didn't write it, did you?" She'd now opened an entire new can of worms. The sisters wouldn't stop until they found the author of the letter. She wondered briefly if that might be a good thing.

"*Nee,* I don't have it with me, but it was very . . . mushy . . . and not something one of *mei* students would have written. At first, I thought maybe Lloyd, Paul, or Henry wrote it, but I've ruled all of them out for various reasons."

"Exactly!" Lizzie screeched. "That's why it has to be Joseph."

"It's not him," Sadie quickly said. "He's been helping me try to find out who penned the note, but it is not him." She thought briefly about how Joseph had lied to her about how he ended up in Indiana. But, as she'd told him, she would have done the same thing to protect a child, especially if that child was her own.

"Don't you worry about a thing," Esther said with the calm voice she was known for. "Lizzie and I will get to the bottom of this."

"And, no matter what you say, it's Joseph." Lizzie gave a taut nod of her head. "It isn't the other men you mentioned. It's that handsome new man."

"He denied writing it, Lizzie," Sadie said as she glanced toward all the women moving toward the kitchen to help with the meal. "And I believe him."

"Tsk, tsk." Lizzie rolled her eyes. "Of course you do, Dear. Esther and I will be by your *haus* tomorrow to lay eyes on this mysterious letter."

Sadie shrugged. "*Ya,* okay. But it isn't Joseph, so you're going to need to really search your minds." Had they forgotten the man was married? Sadie recalled Lizzie's comment about the bishop making an exception and felt it was unlikely.

Joseph couldn't have walked up at a more awkward time. Lizzie and Esther giggled. "*Wie bischt,* Joseph," Lizzie said as she batted her eyes at him.

"Come along, Lizzie," Esther said as she latched onto her sister's arm. "Let's go help in the kitchen." She smiled at Sadie, then winked at Joseph. "Let the young people have some time to themselves."

"I'll be in shortly to help with the meal," Sadie quickly said without looking at Joseph. The women always set out a lovely luncheon after church service, and Sadie didn't want to shirk her responsibilities, but her mind was in a fog.

After the sisters were gone, she turned to Joseph. "I really thought maybe Lizzie or Esther had planted the letter, although they genuinely don't seem to know what I'm talking about." She shrugged. "And it really isn't their style." She groaned. "I'm more confused than ever."

Joseph smiled. "Does it really matter?"

Sadie thought about the mystery, but without it, she recalled again how she wouldn't have grown close to Joseph. "*Nee,* I guess not."

"I was wondering . . ." He stroked his beard. "Leah and I have spent so much time at your *haus.* Would you like to come for supper at our home tonight? You've only been to see us once, and I don't cook a lot, but I can grill a pretty *gut* burger."

"I'd like that," Sadie responded without hesitation, realizing that she could really get to know the Yoders even more deeply by watching them in their own environment, and a change of scenery would be good. After they set a time, Sadie left to go help the women in the kitchen. She had a bounce in her step as she thought about spending the evening with Joseph and Leah. Perhaps this is what God always planned for her because she did trust Joseph, and she adored Leah. The girl would probably benefit from some counseling from the bishop or possibly even an outsider. But, for now, she just wanted to get to know them both even better. Even if all she and Joseph could ever be was friends.

Joseph rounded up Leah as soon as they'd both finished eating. "We've got to go," he told his daughter.

Leah frowned as she glanced at a group of girls talking under a cluster of oak trees. Momentarily, he wondered if he should allow her additional time with her friends since she seemed to be doing better, smiling more, socializing more. "Already?" she finally said in her small voice.

"*Ya,* Butterfly." He lowered himself down to face her. "Sadie is coming for supper tonight. We need to tidy things up. This will be our first guest for a meal."

Leah wrapped her arms around Joseph's neck. "She really is going to be *mei* new *mamm,* isn't she *Daed*?"

It warmed Joseph's heart that Leah was open to the possibility of a family again, one that didn't include violence. They'd turned over a new leaf, but he also couldn't let his daughter believe in something that he didn't believe was possible. "We're just friends, Leah."

His daughter eased away and smiled. "Sadie would be a *gut mamm* because Miriam said that all *mamms* aren't bad."

Joseph's chest tightened. "Remember, we don't want to say too much to others about what happened back at home. We just want to get past it." He knew the girl needed counseling, perhaps some sessions with the bishop. But he wasn't sure if he could trust the bishop here in Montgomery. Would he contact Bishop Zook, Grace's father, and be swayed into thinking that Joseph had hurt his daughter? Would he tell the man where Joseph and Leah are? Would Grace swoop in and take Leah away from him? "Just for now, I think we should not speak of the past. Instead, let's focus on our supper with Sadie tonight."

Leah looked down at the ground, and the sting of the child's harrowing experiences flashed before Joseph's eyes.

But then Leah raised her eyes to his. "Okay. Let's make it a really nice supper so that maybe Sadie will want to be in our family."

How wonderful that sounded to Joseph. But would it be fair to Sadie? No matter the situation, Joseph and Leah were on the run. And there was a chance that they wouldn't be able to stay here. And Joseph wasn't free to give himself to another woman.

Joseph's heart hurt at the thought of having to move Leah again, especially since she was finally beginning to settle in. And so was Joseph. Maybe some secrets were meant to be kept.

Sadie dabbed on a smudge of clear lip gloss, unable to remember the last time she'd done such a thing since it wasn't traditionally allowed. She also sprayed a light mist of lavender-scented essential oil that she'd made a long time ago, thinking she would give it as a gift someday.

She'd never allowed herself to feel giddy until this afternoon. But she trusted Joseph, an unexpected feeling considering his background, the fact that she hadn't known him long, and her own childhood. A person could never have too many friends.

Sadie pulled her buggy onto Joseph's driveway, then knocked on his door right at five, like they had planned. Leah opened the door with a smile on her face.

"You look pretty," Leah said as she stepped aside for Sadie to enter the den.

Sadie had gone to extra effort to iron the wrinkles out of her maroon dress, and there wasn't a strand of hair loose from beneath her prayer covering.

"Danki," she said softly to Leah. "And you look very pretty too." Vanity was frowned

upon, but they were human, and it was obvious that Leah had worked to ready herself for this occasion. Children, so often, wore their prayer coverings lopsided, had smudges of dirt on their faces, or smelled as if they'd been working out in the barn, which most did. Leah was clean as a whistle and glowing. After everything the child had been through, Sadie smiled on the inside too.

"Something smells *gut,*" she said to Joseph when he walked into the room wearing a white short sleeved shirt, untucked, black slacks, and barefooted. He was casually at home in a way she'd never seen him before. After she took in his overall good looks, she tried to recall if she'd ever had a man cook for her. She didn't think so, and most men weren't trained to be handy in the kitchen anyway.

"I hope you like burgers." He chuckled as he gently touched Leah on the shoulder. "We eat a lot of burgers around here. That is . . ." He smiled. ". . . when we aren't eating at your *haus.*"

"I *lieb* burgers," Sadie said as she followed him to the kitchen when he motioned her to do so. Leah latched on to Sadie's hand. "And everything looks lovely." She eyed the three place settings on the kitchen table, along with a jar of chow-chow, bowl of chips, condiments, a plate filled with buns, and three glasses of tea. "This is a treat, having someone cook for me."

"*Daed* is a *gut* cook." Leah sat at the table, then began to count on her fingers. "He makes burgers, and um . . . eggs, and . . . meatloaf, and . . ."

"Basically, just those three meals" Joseph said as he put a platter of burgers on the table before motioning for Sadie to sit across from Leah, while he took the seat at the head of the table.

Following a silent blessing, Joseph held the plate of buns to his left for Sadie. After everyone had a full plate, she took a bite of the burger, then looked at Leah. "You're right. Your daed is a *gut* cook." Smiling at Joseph, she said, "These are very *gut.*"

"*Danki.* Nothing fancy." He smiled back at her.

Feelings of family wrapped around her in a loving protective way, unlike family meals at her house when she'd grown up, always fearful her father would find fault with something her mother had done. Sadie glanced at Leah and wondered if that's how the child had felt around her mother. Leah was young, though, and hopefully this new beginning would wash away some of the memories that the child surely carried.

Habitually, the way they did at her house, they walked to the den after the meal, opting to clean later and have devotions first. A fire in the large stone fireplace would have set the perfect environment, but it was much too warm for that. But she did notice that Joseph had a candle lit on the mantel, which cast a vanilla fragrance throughout the den. He'd gone to a lot of effort.

"I'm going to go to *mei* room and rest," Leah said when devotions were over, adding what appeared to be an exaggerated yawn. She leaned over to Sadie, whom she'd chosen to sit next to on the couch and threw her arms around her. "I'm so glad you're here in our *haus.*"

"I'm happy to be here." Sadie gave Leah a good squeeze before the girl skipped away.

"Hmm . . ." Joseph ran a hand through his hair before he rose from the chair he was sitting in and joined Sadie on the couch. He nudged Sadie with his shoulder and grinned. "She's clearly trying to give us some alone time."

Sadie felt a blush crawling up her cheeks, and even more so when Joseph put a gentle hand on her knee. "I'm happy you're here too," he said.

They'd gotten to know each other, but

always in the comfort of Sadie's surroundings. This was nice, being here, in Joseph and Leah's world. The new life they had created for themselves.

"So, did you decide if you believe the two sisters? Do you still think maybe they placed the secret admirer note on your desk?" He grinned broadly. "In an effort to play matchmaker between the two of us?"

Sadie had told him after worship service about her conversation with Lizzie and Esther. "The more I turn it over in *mei* mind, I just don't think they had anything to do with the note. It's not really their style, and how would they know that we would team up on a hunt to find the author?"

He lifted his hand from her knee and scratched his cheek. "I don't know the women, but it does seem like an odd thing to do."

Sadie waved a dismissive hand in the air. "I'm not going to give it any more thought."

"That's probably for the best. I know you've spent a lot of time worrying about it, and whoever wrote it must have moved on or given up."

"I guess." She sighed. "It still feels odd, but I'm not going to dwell on it anymore."

"The note did serve a purpose." His hand found its way into hers. "It gave me an opportunity to get to know you better, and there's been a huge change in Leah since you came into our lives."

"Speaking of Leah . . ." Joseph stood. "I forgot to put out fresh towels after I took the laundry from the line earlier. I'll be right back."

Sadie tried to envision Joseph hanging clothes on a line. He'd taken on all the roles required to rear his daughter, and despite everything, he'd done a wonderful job. Again, Sadie hoped that Leah's emotional scars would heal, and when the time was right, she would mention to Joseph about possible counseling for Leah with the bishop.

Tonight, she was going to relax into the warm comfort of their company and try not to think about complications. Then she sneezed and sneezed again. After reaching for a handkerchief in her apron and remembering she didn't bring one, she glanced around for a box of tissues. After two more sneezes, she opened the small drawer on the end table next to the couch, recalling that's where her mother always kept a small travel package of tissues.

After she moved a deck of playing cards out of the way, a few pens, and a pad of paper, something caught her eye. And it wasn't tissues.

She glanced to her left to make sure Joseph wasn't coming, then she lifted the focus of her attention, and studied it before placing it back in the drawer.

She stood from the couch, a hand to her racing heart.

"Are you all right?" Joseph walked into the room, but when Sadie opened her mouth to speak, nothing came out.

"Sit down. You're white like a ghost." Joseph reached for her elbow, but she backed away.

"I-I'm so sorry. I'm suddenly not feeling well." She turned to head toward the door, her legs like rubber.

"Wait!" He grabbed her arm, but she yanked it away. "What's wrong? Are you okay to drive your buggy home? I can —"

"*Nee, nee.* I'm fine." Sweat ran the length of her back as she fought not to stutter. "Um, Pl— Please tell Leah I'm sorry I had to leave." She put a hand across her stomach.

"*Ach, nee.* I hope it wasn't *mei* cooking." Joseph's expression was shifting at the same rate as Sadie's emotions, it seemed.

"*Nee. Danki* for supper. We can talk later." She rushed out the door, down the porch steps, and hurriedly backed up her buggy.

She didn't stop shaking until she was out of the driveway.

She silently prayed that Leah would be okay. Sadie repeated the prayer until she was safely home.

Joseph had lied to her, and she'd found the proof in the small drawer in the end table by the couch. If he could so blatantly lie about one thing, who's to say he hadn't lied about everything?

Chapter 18

Joseph closed the door after he'd watched Sadie round the corner as the clippity clop of horse hooves grew fainter, then were gone.

"Where is Sadie?" Leah emerged in her white nightgown. "I thought I heard a buggy leaving."

"Uh, *ya.* Sadie was sick and had to leave early." He sat on the couch, then pulled Leah into a hug when she sat beside him. He kissed her on the top of her head. "She said she was sorry she couldn't wait to tell you goodbye."

Joseph didn't believe Sadie became ill so suddenly and had to leave. Something had shaken her. He'd watched the color drain from her face like an hourglass that had run out of time.

"Do you feel okay?" he asked his daughter on the off chance it had been his food.

"I feel fine, *Daed.*" Leah gazed up at him

with questioning eyes. "Do you?"

"Ya," he said softly, forcing a smile. "I'm sure she'll be fine at school tomorrow. But we need to get you tucked into bed."

Leah lifted herself from the couch when Joseph did, and they shuffled slowly to her bedroom.

Joseph knelt by her bed, and they prayed silently before Joseph tucked her in and extinguished the flame inside the lantern by her bed. "Sleep well, Butterfly. I *lieb* you." He kissed her on the forehead, anxious to be alone with his thoughts.

"I hope Sadie is okay."

"I'm sure she is," Joseph said. "Now, go to sleep." He closed the door behind him, leaving it cracked a little, the way Leah liked it, then he went to the kitchen to face off with the dishes.

As he eased each plate into the soapy water, confusion swirled, but one thing was for sure. Sadie wasn't sick, and Joseph racked his mind to recall what he could have said to upset her. Her lip had been trembling, like she was scared.

But all he'd done was go get Leah a fresh hand towel for when she brushed her teeth later. Prior to that, everything had been fine.

Joseph would confront her about it tomorrow. Tonight, he wasn't sure he would sleep well with this hanging between them. Unsure what it was made things even worse.

It was a couple of hours later when Sadie got into bed and snuggled deep beneath the covers with only her eyes peeking above her quilt. She'd memorized the flow of the tree shadows that glided into the room at dusk, usually swaying outside her bedroom window in a rhythm that put her to sleep. Tonight, there was a darkness within the shadows, as if the world were keeping a secret from her.

Her trust had been tried and tested in the past, and Sadie had always felt her way through the dense confusion and reached a clearing. Now, she wasn't sure she'd ever unravel the betrayal that encircled her like a web of deceit manipulated to fit her perfectly. She'd been drawn in like an unsuspecting insect by a predator.

Seeing a copy of the secret admirer's letter in the drawer at Joseph's house still had her blinking her eyes and wondering if she'd seen a phantom piece of paper, a vision that tricked her into thinking she was losing touch with reality. But she was sure that it was an exact copy of the secret admirer letter. Joseph had apparently written her the letter and kept a copy for himself.

But why?

Her mind had raced through every possible scenario, and she'd finally landed on the one that made the most sense; Joseph had planned all along to help her search for the author of the letter, his way of getting close to her. *Lizzie and Esther were right.* And that revelation, combined with Joseph's troublesome past, left Sadie wondering what her next move should be. *So many lies from a man I can't be with anyway.*

She could distance herself from Joseph, but what about Leah? There was no doubt that Leah was fond of Sadie, and Sadie cared for the little girl.

Sadie's biggest problem was that someone had abused Leah. Had it been Joseph all along? Leah seemed comfortable with her father, and he was devoted to her.

As she struggled to drift off to sleep, she decided to turn this over to God. Only He could provide her the answers she needed and a way to protect Leah.

Her last thoughts were of that precious child with a vision of the milk scene in Sadie's kitchen. Looking back, Joseph had reacted harshly. He had easily explained away his actions, but had Sadie been fooled? Tomorrow, she would question Leah and get the truth.

■ ■ ■ ■

Joseph paced in the darkness of his bedroom, the flame of his lantern barely flickering as he repeatedly stroked his beard. Something had spooked Sadie. That much he knew for sure.

He tiptoed from his room and made his way to the den, folding his arms across his chest as he looked around. He sat on the couch and flipped through the magazines on the coffee table. She'd seen the ones about hunting and hadn't seemed disturbed. Not everyone agreed with the practice of shooting animals, but Joseph had always believed that if you ate your kill, it was all right in the eyes of God.

After he sat down on the couch, he leaned his head back against the cushion and sighed. He wished he hadn't allowed himself to care for Sadie so much. Dormant feelings had risen to the surface, but more importantly than his own feelings were his daughter's. Leah didn't just adore Sadie, she'd practically adopted her as a mother. Things were happening much too fast in a situation that could never render a good outcome. Perhaps that recollection had slapped Sadie upside the head, and she'd chosen to spare herself any heartache that might be forthcoming.

Nee. Joseph shook his head as his thoughts rolled back around to her abrupt and awkward exit. Something had shifted Sadie's thoughts, feelings, and actions. And Joseph had no idea what could have happened. His marital status had always been a dark shadow that hovered around any developing feelings. This felt like something else.

He stood, sighed again, then headed back to his bedroom. He would confront Sadie first thing in the morning when he took Leah to school.

Sadie arrived earlier than usual after praying late into the night that she would do right by Leah, whatever that meant. Somehow, she needed to protect Leah but also detach from Joseph, and that would be tricky. She would start by not going outside of the one-room schoolhouse to greet the children as they arrived. That way, Joseph wouldn't have an opportunity to corner her and press for answers. Sadie didn't even know what the questions were in his mind or hers. It was a jumbled scenario fraught with outcomes that must be handled correctly.

"*Wie bischt,* Miriam," she said to Lloyd's

daughter. Sadie's decisions could indirectly influence Miriam since she'd become good friends with Leah. *So much to consider.*

After Miriam had taken her seat, Sadie stayed inside the doorway and greeted the other children. Her stomach clenched when she saw Joseph walking her way and holding Leah's hand. "*Gut* morning, Leah." Sadie avoided Joseph's piercing glare as she greeted his daughter and instructed her to take her seat.

"What happened last night?" Joseph said in a whisper as several children slipped by them. "And don't tell me nothing because something spooked you, and you didn't even act like yourself when you rushed to leave."

Sadie had a strict rule about lying, but a partial version of the truth would have to do. "My stomach was suddenly upset, and I felt the need to get home." She slowly lifted her eyes to his, wishing she hadn't, as visions of kissing him fought to smother more important issues. "I'm sorry."

She'd felt a shield of protection from Joseph, something she had trusted. Now she was reminded why it wasn't safe to trust any man. Her heart pounded in her chest as temptation crept over her, the desire to question him directly about the copy of the note. But now wasn't the time. His expression was drawn, his eyebrows furrowed, and his eyes angry. She didn't want to do this in front of the children. "Can we talk after school?" As much as she didn't want to face him regarding any of this, she would have to.

"Ya." His expression softened, eyes moistening. "And I hope you'll tell me the truth because I don't think a stomachache caused you to bolt from *mei haus* the way you did. Something else is wrong, and I hope we can talk our way through it." He gently put a hand on her arm, an inappropriate gesture considering the children who were present. She took a step back, and Joseph dropped his arm to his side, then sighed. "Okay, I'll see you after school."

Sadie nodded. She would tell Joseph about the note, that she no longer trusted him, and that she could only be a friend to Leah via their relationship as teacher/student. That part tore at her heart as much as giving up any potential relationship with Joseph. *He's married anyway. I should have never kissed him.*

Following morning devotions, Sadie made her way around the room, checking to see that each child was studying his or her notebook based on her instructions yesterday.

The kindergarten children were coloring pictures with coordinating numbers. Levels one through three were matching English words with Pennsylvania Dutch, and her older students were reading a novel that had been pre-approved by the bishop. Sadie felt she should have the final say on what the students read, that her years as a teacher and wisdom should be trusted, but the bishop and elders always wanted to know what the children would be reading.

As the clock on the wall ticked, Sadie's dread grew. How would Joseph react when Sadie told him she had seen the note? Would he accuse her of snooping when she was only in search of a tissue? Did it matter? Sadie believed that God orchestrated such events to help her put the pieces of this mismatched puzzle together.

A gentle tap on the door drew her from her thoughts. "Keep working, children," she said as she walked to the door. There was still an hour of school left, so she couldn't imagine who it might be. Perhaps it was Henry alerting her to a plumbing problem or some other issue. Although Henry had been keeping his distance, seemingly sulking with his head down and avoiding Sadie, and that was okay.

But it wasn't Henry.

Sadie opened the door and stepped outside onto the covered porch since she didn't recognize this woman. "*Wie bischt.* Can I help you?" She eyed the Amish woman dressed in a dark green dress with a black apron. Sadie knew everyone in their community, or so she'd thought. There were also only a handful of women with blonde hair like her own, and this woman had golden hair tucked neatly beneath her prayer covering. As was tradition, she had no makeup on, but Sadie noticed right away that her eyes were moist. In her hand, she held an envelope.

"*Mei* name is Grace." The woman clasped her hands in front of her, clutching the envelope. "Grace Yoder. I'm Leah's *mudder,* and I'm here to pick her up."

Sadie stopped breathing before she found her breath and responded. "What?" Joseph had told her that Leah's mother had left the Amish faith, but this woman was in full Amish attire and spoke with a hint of Pennsylvania Dutch, the way most of their people did.

Grace blinked her moist eyes as she pushed the envelope toward Sadie. "I have traveled here from Pennsylvania. *Mei* husband, Joseph, chose to leave our community, and with the help of our bishop,

I've been able to track him here. He has been on the run with our daughter, Leah." She covered her face with her hands, sniffling.

Sadie opened the envelope and pulled out a folded one-page document that had been prepared by an English lawyer in Pennsylvania. There was some legal language that wasn't clear to Sadie, but one part stuck out in bold type. **GRACE YODER HAS LEGAL CUSTODY OF LEAH YODER AND UPON REUNITING, LEAH IS TO BE TURNED OVER TO HER MOTHER IMMEDIATELY.**

Sadie's first reaction was to call Joseph, but he kept his phone off during the day, as most of their members did, unless there was the threat of a potential emergency. Sadie spent a few moments trying to decipher if this was an emergency or a blessing. Either way, Leah would be the one to suffer if she didn't get to say goodbye to her father, no matter the circumstances.

This was all new to Sadie. She'd never dealt with English legalities.

"Joseph has brainwashed Leah into believing that their being on the run is a healthy way for a child to live." Grace sniffled before retrieving a handkerchief from her apron pocket. She dabbed at her eyes. "Leah belongs at home with the people who know and *lieb* her."

Despite the niggling in her gut that she should speak with Joseph before handing over Leah to a stranger, the first thing she'd need to see is how Leah reacted to this news. She'd mentioned on several occasions that she missed her mother. Joseph had explained to Sadie that Leah did miss her mother, the good times they'd had, but that she also missed a mother figure, someone to fulfill motherly duties like cooking, cleaning, and nurturing.

This had to be God's answer to Sadie's prayers the night before.

"I'll get Leah," Sadie finally said as she forced a smile and turned to go back into the schoolhouse, closing the door behind her.

She lowered herself down by Leah's desk. "Leah." Sadie waited until the child's eyes met with hers, not wanting to miss any part of her reaction. She silently prayed that Leah wouldn't cry, scream, want her father, or make a scene in front of the other children. Sadie was crying enough on the inside for both. *I will miss you, sweet girl.*

The niggling that Joseph should at least know about this wouldn't go away, but Sadie also couldn't fight the English law. It was surprising that Grace had gone to a lawyer. She'd obviously returned to the Amish way of life — or never left in the first place. But most of their people shied away from English legalities. But it had happened a few times.

Leah blinked her eyes at Sadie. "Am I in trouble?"

Sadie quickly shook her head. "*Nee,* sweetheart. You are not in trouble. But your *mudder* is here to pick you up." She tried to smile even though her heart was shattered. "She's missed you and is ready to take you home."

Sadie thought about all the lies Joseph had told her — how Grace had left their community, abandoned their way of life, and prior to that . . . inappropriately disciplined their daughter. The woman standing outside with her demure posture and soft-spoken voice didn't fit the description of what Joseph had explained.

Still watching Leah carefully, Sadie said, "Are you ready to go home to Pennsylvania?"

Tears rolled down the girl's cheeks, adding more cracks to Sadie's already broken heart. "Does she want to hug me? And what about *Daed*? And I thought you liked *mei daed*? I thought we were going to be a family." Leah's voice became louder as she spoke through her tears.

Sadie glanced around the room. Every pair of eyes was on her and Leah, and Sadie wished that wasn't the case. "Let's go outside and see your *mudder.* We can talk this through." She stood and offered Leah her hand.

Leah took Sadie's hand and shuffled toward the door with her head down, but she stopped at Miriam's desk. "Bye, Miriam."

Miriam looked up at her friend with moist eyes. "Bye, Leah."

Even though they were only children, there were enough unspoken words to fill the room with an air of sadness that Sadie was sure everyone felt. She gave the girls a few moments of silent communication before she eased Leah back into step with her.

Sadie opened the door just as Grace squatted down, still crying. "*Mei* sweet *maedel,* I've missed you. Give your *mudder* a hug."

Leah did as her mother instructed and put her arms around her neck. It was stiff and unnatural, but that was probably because Leah hadn't seen the woman in so long. Joseph had filled her mind with thoughts that weren't true. And Leah didn't seem afraid of Grace, which should have been the case if the woman had abused her.

Sadie's bottom lip trembled, knowing she would be saying goodbye to Leah shortly. She'd also have to tell Joseph about finding the note at his house, about Grace showing up, and how all of Joseph's lies have caught up with him. Still, somewhere deep within her heart, she knew Joseph would be hurting. But things needed to happen in a way that was best for Leah, and Grace had the documents to prove it. Plus, Sadie had prayed hard for a good outcome for Leah.

Even without any children of her own, Sadie now realized that a child could break her heart as badly as any man. Sadie felt shattered as Leah walked away holding her mother's hand. Leah didn't look back. Sadie couldn't stop watching.

CHAPTER 19

Joseph flicked the reins to pick up speed on the way to the school. He was anxious to talk to Sadie. Whatever had shaken her, he had to know so he could fix it. She'd become so important to him. He hadn't thought he would ever fall in love in again, but Sadie had slowly been chipping away at the barrier he had cemented around his heart. More than ever, he wanted things to be right between them even if his marriage prevented them from being more than friends. He had racked his brain to figure out what he could have done for her to act so strangely the night before.

He tethered his horse to one of the hitching posts in front of the school. There were two other buggies with parents also waiting, but they were all early. He had decided to wait until everyone had left the school, despite being anxious. His chat with Sadie should be private.

Leah was usually one of the first children to run out to the buggy, but when other parents began to leave with their sons and daughters — and still no Leah — Joseph stepped out of his buggy and started toward the door of the schoolhouse where Sadie was standing, her hands folded in front of her. Henry was around the corner, cleaning the glass windows. Joseph really didn't want him to overhear his conversation with Sadie, but his chest tightened the closer he got to Sadie . . . and still no Leah.

"Where is *mei* daughter?" He tried to conceal the panic rambling around his insides. "She's usually outside by now."

He waited until he was right in front of Sadie before he asked again. "Where is Leah?"

Sadie took a deep breath. "Joseph, Leah's *mudder* picked her up today."

Joseph slapped a hand to his forehead as his heart plummeted. "What?" He grabbed both of Sadie's arms. "Please tell me this isn't true! I've told you about Leah's *mudder.*"

Sadie wiggled out of his grasp as she scowled. "Don't talk to me about truth!" She glared at him, but Joseph didn't care about her worries now. "Besides, Grace had legal documents that proved she was Leah's guardian."

Joseph bent at the waist, his hands on his knees, as he stared at his black work boots, trying to assimilate this information and figure out what he was going to do. He straightened and glared into the woman's eyes who had just ruined Leah's life. "How could you do this? How could you? I told you that Grace left our community, that she had taken up with an *Englisch* man, and that before that, she hadn't treated Leah *gut.*" He pointed his finger at her. "She finally tracks us down, then you hand over Leah without a thought in the world! What kind of person are you?"

She pushed his finger away from her. "Don't you dare ask me what type of person I am. First, Grace was dressed as an Amish woman, and as I said, she had the necessary paperwork. And I no longer believe anything you say! Do you hear me?"

Joseph lifted his shoulders and raised his palms. "I know something happened last night that is making you act this way, but I have no idea what. And, honestly, I don't care right now. You just handed over *mei* daughter to a woman who will discipline her in a way that is inappropriate! I can't win legally because of her father. Do you think I like being on the run? But I will do whatever I must to protect Leah!"

"You wrote the secret admirer letter!" Sadie yelled. "Then you pretended to be *mei* friend, lying all the while, helping me search for a man who doesn't exist. You wrote the letter. And if you would lie about something like that, why should I trust anything you say? It was all manipulation to get close to me!"

"You've lost your mind." He put a hand to his forehead, blocking the late afternoon sun. "Was she in a car or buggy?" Joseph latched on to both of Sadie's arms, firm enough that she wouldn't wiggle away. "Please, I'm begging you. Which way did they go?"

"I didn't see," she said. "They went around to the other side of the building. But I think I heard a car engine." She groaned. "Now, let go. You're hurting me."

Hurting Sadie physically or emotionally was the last thing he wanted to do, but there was a panic stirring inside of him that wouldn't be stifled until he found Leah. He released his grip on her and pressed his palms together. "*Ach,* Dear Heavenly Father, please direct me to Leah, and forgive Sadie for what she doesn't understand." Joseph fought tears as he began to pace on the porch of the small schoolhouse. "Why would you think I wrote the letter, Sadie? Why would I lie to you about something like that? I did not write you a letter, and all *mei* intentions to help you were genuine. But now I've lost Leah, and she is in danger, whether you believe that or not."

"When you went for clean towels last night for Leah, I was looking for a tissue. I opened the small drawer in the end table by the couch since that's where *mei mudder* used to keep tissues." She paused, her lip trembling. "There was a copy of the letter in the drawer, the exact letter that was on *mei* desk."

"I didn't write it." Joseph racked his brain. "Leah keeps her things in that drawer, extra pens, pencils . . ." He paused. "But she couldn't have written it. She doesn't have that kind of vocabulary."

"*Mei* thoughts exactly," Sadie said as Joseph began to scan the grounds around the school. "And why would Leah choose to go with her *mudder* if she is mean to her? She willingly went into her arms!"

Joseph groaned as he shook his head and stared at Sadie. "Did Grace say, 'give your *mudder* a hug'?

"Uh . . . yes." Sadie scratched her cheek as a perplexed expression began to spread across her face.

"Think back. Did Leah embrace her back?"

"*Nee.* Not really. Maybe a little." Sadie chewed her bottom lip. "But it wasn't like she tried to run away from her. She walked by her side to either a car or a buggy on the other side of the building. As I said, I think a car."

"That's because 'give your *mudder* a hug' means 'hug me or else'."

Sadie shook her head so hard that strands of hair fell from her prayer covering, then she placed her palms on either side of her head. "I'd never do anything to put Leah in danger."

"But you did!" Joseph's grief left him unable to sympathize.

"*Ach, nee . . .* I'm confused. I saw the letter, and I just assumed that you wrote it and kept a copy." Sadie blinked back tears. "But she looked so Amish, spoke softly and with kindness. She said you stole Leah illegally."

"You already knew that." Joseph lowered his head. "And now I have no way to protect Leah." He glared at Sadie. "Grace doesn't even like *kinner.*"

Sadie couldn't stop the tears that rolled down her cheek. No matter who wrote the letter, Joseph's grief over losing his daughter was real. He truly feared for her safety.

Now, so did she.

"If she doesn't like *kinner,* why would she even want Leah back?" she asked him, choking out the words.

"I must try to find her. Maybe she hasn't left town yet."

Joseph jogged to his buggy, and like his daughter . . . he never looked back. Were they both out of Sadie's life? Her heart constricted in a way that made it hard for her to breathe. Then she silently prayed that Leah would be okay.

"Where could they be?" she said to herself aloud as she took up pacing the same path Joseph had on the front porch.

Sadie thought Grace had arrived in a car. *Why didn't I go look?* Since she'd arrived from Pennsylvania, or anywhere else but Montgomery, Indiana, she would likely be in a car. They could be on their way to an airport, a bus, or driving across the country.

She might not understand about the letter, but she recalled Joseph's panicked expressions, and she'd seen the hurt in his eyes that she hadn't believed him.

Henry rounded the corner. "Are you all right? I tried not to eavesdrop, but it was hard not to hear Joseph yelling."

Sadie stopped pacing and sighed. *"Ya."* She didn't want to tell Henry what was going on, but she wondered how much he had overheard. "It's Leah. She left school with a woman that she probably shouldn't have, but I didn't know any better."

Henry tipped back the rim of his straw hat before he looped his thumbs beneath his suspenders and walked up the porch steps until he was standing right in front of her. Ever since his words and actions during their meeting, she'd felt uncomfortable around Henry, but she reminded herself that, prior to that, they'd always been friends.

"Why did you let Leah go with her?" Henry's voice wasn't accusatory, but he locked eyes with her in a way that made her look away, almost like he was testing her.

"I-I don't know." Sadie threw her hands up. "There's been a lot going on, and I-I'm confused about . . . some things." She heard the shakiness in her voice.

Henry took off his hat and wiped an arm across his sweaty forehead. Summer had snuck up on them before spring had officially bid farewell.

He put his hat back on, then locked eyes with Sadie again. "I'm not sure if I should get involved with this." He stroked his chin, with only a shadow of a day's beard. "But . . ." He scowled. "If you think Leah could be in danger, I might know where she is."

Sadie's chest tightened. "Where? And how would you know something like that?"

Henry tipped his head to one side. "Didn't you recognize the woman?"

"Nee." Sadie was sure she'd never seen her. "There are only a couple of women, other than me, with blonde hair in our community. I would have remembered."

Henry inched closer. "Picture her with lots of makeup and without Amish clothing."

Sadie tried to envision the woman who took Leah in the way Henry described. Then she covered her mouth with her hand and gasped. "*Nee,* it can't be."

Henry raised an eyebrow.

"Gretchen?" Sadie made the connection. The flashy woman with lots of makeup whom Henry had spent time with. "Your Gretchen?"

He frowned. "She's not *mei* Gretchen."

"Why would she pretend to be Amish? Or was she pretending to be Gretchen?" Sadie shook her head. "Either way, is she really Leah's *mudder*?" She grabbed Henry's arm, much the same way Joseph had held hers. "Do you know where they are?"

"As far as I know, she's Leah's mother. And *ya* . . . I have an idea where they might be."

Sadie let go of his arm. "Did you know that she was planning to kidnap Leah?"

"Wait a minute. I think *kidnap* is a strong word. She has legal papers that say she has custody of Leah." Henry shrugged. "It wasn't really *mei* business."

"Well, it's your business now because I think Gretchen might harm Leah." Sadie paused as guilt flooded over her. She stomped her foot. "You should have told me about this, Henry."

He shrugged again despite the immediacy of their situation. "You haven't exactly been yourself lately."

She assumed he was referring to their meeting when he'd caught her off guard with some of his comments. "I could say the same about you, Henry." She lowered her eyebrows at him, which brought on another shrug.

Sadie peeked inside the schoolroom to make sure all the children had been picked up by a parent. "Take me to where you think Grace — or Gretchen — might be," she demanded.

He nodded. "But you should probably know that she can be unpleasant at times.

She might not welcome you, and she's surely going to be mad at me."

"I don't care." She scurried down the porch steps in the direction of her buggy. "Come on." Then she stopped and turned around. "Can we get there by buggy?"

"Ya," Henry said before he began to follow her down the steps, then across the grounds of the schoolyard.

Sadie huffed as she untethered her horse. "Joseph said she doesn't like *kinner* and didn't want a *boppli* to begin with. Why would she even want Leah?"

"I can answer that." Henry sighed. "I'll tell you on the way."

Sadie latched onto the reins and quickly backed up her buggy. "Tell me." She held her breath as she waited.

Chapter 20

Hours later, Joseph had covered as much of Montgomery, Indiana, as he could, stopping only to give his horse water and rest. He didn't even know what he was looking for. A car, presumably, which would be like finding a needle in a haystack. Could Grace be riding around in a buggy again? As he pulled up at his house, he sat in his buggy, closed his eyes, and recalled a time when they rode around together, attended worship, and then welcomed Leah into their lives. It wasn't long before Joseph began to recognize that Grace might not be cut out for motherhood, and he often blamed himself for pushing her into having a child so soon. She'd gotten pregnant three months after they were married, and she was young . . . eighteen.

But when she decided to leave the community, she left everything — him, Leah, and their way of life. He couldn't figure out why Grace kept hunting him and Leah down when she didn't want them to be a family. He also didn't know what paperwork Grace was in possession of, or if it was as fake is she is.

Regrets would bog a man down, and Joseph knew that. But it didn't stop him from lowering his head and crying. It was nonproductive, and he couldn't sit idle right now. He forced himself to go inside.

After getting a glass of iced tea and letting his horse have a longer rest, he headed back out. He was losing hope that he would find Grace and Leah, and he feared for Leah. He doubted Grace's parenting skills had improved.

Joseph picked up the pace. He'd look for his daughter until his horse couldn't go anymore.

"You think she's in there?" Sadie pulled the buggy to a stop in front of a very old motel on the outskirts of town. "Why would you . . ." Then it hit her. "Oh," she said, assuming this must be where Henry used to meet Gretchen.

Henry had shared what he knew on the way about Grace, that she wanted money.

"If Grace is holding Leah hostage so that Joseph will give her money, it will not work out well. I don't think he has any. He's been doing work at *mei* place." She shook her head at the information Henry had shared. "And what a horrible thing to do, hold a child like this and demand money."

Henry sighed. "I know, but that's what she told me. Not in those exact words, but that she needed money, and if Joseph couldn't give her any, that she would take Leah back to Pennsylvania. She said her parents would be more inclined to help her if she brought Leah back."

Sadie sat quietly, thinking, trying to formulate her sentences without revealing too much. "Did Gretchen — Grace, I guess — ever say anything about Leah? Did she say she missed her? It's also hard for me to understand how a mother can walk away from a child." When Henry just shook his head, Sadie said, "Do you think she would ever harm Leah?" She held her breath and hoped that Henry would tell her that deep down Grace was a good person and would never harm a child.

"I don't know," he said as he avoided looking at Sadie. "She mentioned once that *kinner* were a nuisance, loud, and demanded strict discipline."

Sadie shuddered, then pointed to a small building that was attached to a long row of rooms. "There's the office. Do you think they will tell us if Grace is in one of the rooms?" She scanned the parking lot. *No buggies.* "Do you recognize any of these cars?"

"Nee." Henry shifted his weight in the seat of the buggy as he began to nervously rub his hands together.

"Despite everything . . ." Sadie scowled. "I thought Joseph said she left him for another man. Could that man be inside?"

Henry shook his head. "*Nee,* she traveled from Pennsylvania by herself. She took a plane, then rented a car." He looked around the parking lot. "But I don't see the blue car she used before."

Sadie was trembling from head to toe. "Joseph should be here."

Henry was quiet.

"How could you let this happen, Henry?" Sadie swiped at her eyes. "I've always known you to be a *gut* man." Shaking her head, she went on. "Gretchen doesn't seem like someone you would take up with."

He scowled as he glared at her. "I know nothing about Joseph. Gretchen told me he was abusive to his daughter, that he was on the run with her, and that he owed her money. I had no reason at the time not to trust her. And, honestly, how do we know which one of them is telling the truth?" He stepped out of the buggy. "But I'm going to go see if the clerk in the office will tell me if Gretchen is here." He lowered his head before he looked back up at Sadie. "She knows me. I've been here before."

Sadie heard the regret in his voice, so instead of reprimanding him further, she nodded. She gasped when she remembered her cell phone in the small console of her buggy. She rarely used it, and she wasn't even sure if it was charged. As she fumbled to turn it on, she saw that she had very little battery life. Even though mobile phones were mostly for emergencies, she assumed Joseph would have his turned on. She found Joseph's number and called. He answered on the first ring.

"I've been trying to call you, but your phone has been off. Did you find Leah?" His voice was fraught with worry, and once again, she believed his story over Gretchen's.

"Maybe. Henry and I are at the motel where Henry used to meet Gretchen . . . I mean Grace. He is checking with the clerk in the office."

"Where?" Joseph's voice was frantic.

Sadie told him the name of the motel and explained where it was located.

"I'm about fifteen minutes from there by buggy. I'm on *mei* way."

He hung up before Sadie could say anything else, but her pulse picked up when she saw Henry walking back to the buggy, and he was nodding his head. He leaned his head inside the small window of the buggy. "She's in room 103."

Sadie willed her pulse to slow down. "Joseph is on his way."

Henry opened the door and sat, leaving the door ajar. "I guess we should wait for him. If we go in, Gretchen might jump in a car with Leah, take off, and Joseph will have no chance to reclaim his daughter." He cut his eyes at Sadie. "If what you're saying is true."

"I believe him, Henry. I wasn't sure at first because of . . ." She thought better about mentioning the letter. ". . . because I don't know him that well." It wasn't true. In some ways, she felt like she'd known Joseph forever. But trust was such a big issue for her that she'd found it hard to believe she was falling in love with him even if it was a forbidden love. And she was quick to dismiss him when she believed that he had lied to her. *If anything happens to Leah . . .* Sadie cringed. That little girl took priority over everything, and Sadie wasn't going to calm down until she saw for herself that she was okay.

"Did you hear that?" Henry straightened in the seat and cupped a hand behind his ear. "Listen."

Sadie held her breath, and what she heard caused her skin to crawl. "It sounded like a scream coming from that room. We must go in," she said as she began to cry.

Henry bolted from the buggy and jogged toward room 103.

On shaky legs, Sadie ran behind him across the parking lot, both stopping at the dingy red door with paint peeling and the number 3 hanging sideways.

Henry banged hard on the door with one fist. "Gretchen, it's me. Open the door."

Sadie shook from head to toe, wishing Joseph was here. "Leah are you in there?" she yelled at the top of her lungs.

Then she heard whimpering. A child's cry. "Henry, do something," she said barely above a whisper. "Do something. *Please.*"

"Gretchen, open the door. Now!" Henry beat on the door again.

"Go away, Henry! I told you we are done. Now just leave before I call the police."

Sadie could feel the color draining from her face. She'd never had any reason to call the police or be involved with them. Her people avoided outsiders, but for the first time in her life, she was considering it. "What should we do?"

As she waited for Henry to respond, a horse and buggy pulled into the parking lot and stopped abruptly. Sadie put a hand to her forehead, blocking the sun as a man sprung from the buggy and ran toward her.

"Move!" Joseph's booming voice rattled in Sadie's ear as Joseph eased her aside. Then with all his weight, he threw his shoulder against the door, and it flew open.

Chapter 21

Joseph was taken aback momentarily when he laid eyes upon his former wife, dressed in a dark green Amish dress, but when he saw Leah hovering in the corner with a red slap mark across her face, he rushed to his daughter, picked her up, and held her against his chest. "What have you done?" he yelled at Grace.

"Don't act so high and mighty, Joseph. Did our parents not discipline us for speaking out of turn?" She pointed to him and Leah. "She is a smarty pants and doesn't know how to speak properly to adults. She told me I was a bad *mudder* and that she already had another *mudder.*" Grace looked Sadie up and down. "Are you the supposed other *mudder*?"

Despite her leaving, Joseph heard the remnants of Pennsylvania Dutch in Grace's voice. He looked at Sadie. She was trembling, her eyes moist, and her mouth was open, but she didn't speak. He caught sight of a big red suitcase and recognized it as the same luggage Grace had left with six months prior.

To Joseph's surprise, Leah wiggled out of his arms, then ran to Sadie, who lowered herself to embrace his child in her protective arms while kissing her on the cheek. "You're safe," she whispered.

Leah clung to Sadie with both arms around her neck as the child gently sobbed, her face buried against her chest. Joseph couldn't hear whatever else Sadie was whispering to his daughter. He refocused on Grace.

"I don't care what type of legal papers you have, Grace. You aren't taking Leah away." He could feel his face turning red as his nostrils flared.

She pointed to Henry, who had a phone in his hands that must have been in his pocket. "Call the police." She eyed her own phone on a nearby table. "Mine is dead."

Joseph shifted his glare to Henry. He didn't know this man, only what Sadie had told him, and he didn't have any idea how deeply Grace might have her claws into Henry. But the man lowered his head, shook it, then looked back at Grace.

"I'm not calling the police, Gretchen. I

don't care what kind of legal documents you have." He nodded to Leah, who was still clinging to Sadie. "You slapped that child across the face. And you just admitted it." He paused, sighing. "And I suspect it isn't the first time based on the way Leah is reacting."

"I've told you about Joseph!" Grace pointed to him, her face fire-red. "He is the one who isn't a *gut* parent."

Henry locked eyes with Joseph. "Take Sadie and Leah and leave."

The man spoke with an authority that Joseph wasn't sure should be heeded. "Then what?" he asked.

"I'll handle this." Henry glanced at Sadie and Leah before looking back at Joseph. "Just get them out of here."

"Nee!" Grace attempted to dive for Leah, but Henry blocked her with his arm.

"Gretchen, let them leave. You and I need to have a little talk." Henry kept his arm out, blocking her.

Joseph nodded at Sadie, who stood, then scooped Leah into her arms, then Joseph followed Sadie and his daughter to the door. Before he exited, he turned to Henry. "Are you sure?"

Henry nodded with an unspoken clarity that he was going to take care of this situation. Joseph chose to trust him and nodded back at him.

After they were outside the room, Joseph took Leah from Sadie's arms and held her tightly before easing her away to examine her face.

"I'm okay, *Daed.*" Her tiny voice left a hole in Joseph's heart, one he hoped he could fill by making this horrible experience up to his daughter . . . somehow.

Sadie stood speechless, her heart still pounding in her chest, unsure of what to do. She and Joseph had spoken so harshly to each other, and they both had buggies in the parking lot. She wanted to be with him and Leah, but she couldn't leave her horse here. And what about Henry? Despite his recent actions, she'd always known their groundskeeper to be a good man. Would he be safe alone with Grace?

"Danki," Joseph said to her with tears in his eyes before she could process what was happening any further. "Can you please come to our *haus*? I think we have things to talk about."

Sadie opened her mouth to tell him that she wanted to go home, that they could talk later. She was overwhelmed emotionally and concerned about what was happening inside the motel room with Henry and Gretchen. But then Leah lifted her head from her father's shoulder.

"Please, come, Sadie." The child sniffled. "Please."

Sadie glanced at Joseph, then Leah, both with pleading eyes. "*Ya,* okay," she said. "I will follow you in *mei* buggy."

During the route, Sadie had a lot to think about. How quickly she'd turned on Joseph when she'd believed him to be so sincere. *But the copy of the note.* And what about Leah? The poor child had chosen Sadie as her mother right in front of her real mother. *But what is a real mother?* Not someone who slaps a six-year-old hard enough to leave a red whelp on her face.

She owed Joseph an apology, but where should they go from here? They'd behaved badly to each other, and Leah was caught in the middle. Even a friendship between them seemed to hang in the balance.

She pulled into Joseph's driveway right behind him. Leah jumped out of the buggy and ran to Sadie, hugging her around the knees. The knot in Sadie's throat felt permanent. Sadie couldn't be Leah's mother. She'd barely begun a relationship with the girl's father — a relationship that could never be the type Leah hoped for.

"I'm going to get some ice for Leah's face," Joseph said after he hung his hat on the rack by the door before rushing past them to the kitchen.

Leah hurried to the couch and motioned for Sadie to sit by her. Leah's left cheek was swelling, and she'd probably have a black eye tomorrow.

"I've got coffee percolating," Joseph said as he reentered the den and handed Leah a towel with ice inside. "Keep this against your face as much as you can." The pained expression on Joseph's face kept Sadie's knot in her throat perfectly in place. "I'll be right back with the coffee." He left the room again with a hand to his forehead, and Sadie's heart ached for him also.

"Miriam said all *mudders* don't hit." Leah gazed up at Sadie with the ice to her cheek, her eyes moist with tears.

Sadie tried unsuccessfully to swallow. She cleared her throat instead. "That's right, all *mudders* don't hit. I'm sure lots of *kinner* get spankings, but there are correct ways to discipline a child." She paused. "Leah, you are safe now."

Leah laid her head on Sadie's shoulder, and Sadie put an arm around her, pulling her closer. Leah lifted her head. "You'd never hit like that, would you? And I know how *gut* a cook you are. And you're smart about things."

Sadie sighed. She knew where Leah was going with this. "*Nee,* I would never hit like that." She forced a smile. "And *danki* for the compliments about *mei* cooking and teaching."

Joseph walked into the room. He placed a cup of coffee on the small table in front of Sadie and Leah, along with a glass of milk for his daughter and a plate of cookies, then he took a seat in the rocking chair on the other side of the room and just stared at them. The look in his eyes was one of pained relief, and Sadie thought she saw a glimpse of his soul. *How could I have doubted him?*

She glanced out the window when the propane light came on in the yard. Lots of time had passed since school let out, and soon it would be dark.

Leah stood from where she was sitting beside Sadie, walked to her father with the ice on her face, and said, *"Daed,* please make Sadie *mei mamm."*

Joseph almost smiled for the first time since she'd seen him. "I think Sadie and I have some things to talk about." He glanced at Sadie. "But you never know how things might work out."

Sadie felt despair, despite his statement.

Maybe he wasn't still furious with her now that Leah was safely home, but Leah's request wasn't one they could fulfill.

"Is it okay for me to pray that Sadie can become *mei mamm*?" Leah tipped her tiny head to one side as she kept the ice pressed to her cheek.

"I think it's okay to pray about whatever is on your heart." He kissed Leah on the forehead. "Maybe a hot bath would make you feel better, and we can talk more later." Glancing at Sadie, he said, "I need to talk to Sadie."

Leah nodded and smiled. After she'd rounded the corner, Sadie covered her face with her hands and cried. She couldn't hold it in any longer. "I'm so sorry. I'm so very sorry. When I think about what could have happened . . ."

She felt a strong arm pulling her close when Joseph sat beside her. "But Leah is okay, and I'm sorry too. I reacted so harshly."

"I deserved it, Joseph. I should have known that you could never harm Leah. It's just that trust comes so hard for me, and when I saw a copy of the secret admirer letter in your drawer . . ." She nodded to the drawer. "I believed with all *mei* heart that you had written it and kept a copy. I wasn't completely clear as to your intentions, but I didn't even give you a chance to explain, and I almost let Leah get hauled away by her mother."

Joseph quickly removed his arm, stood, and walked to the drawer on the other side of where Sadie was sitting. He jerked it open and began rummaging around until he took out the folded piece of paper that Sadie had seen. As he read it, his forehead crinkled, and then he scratched his cheek. "I'm so confused. Leah keeps miscellaneous things in this drawer." He read the letter, then looked at Sadie. "Do you have a copy machine at the schoolhouse?"

"*Nee.* We would need electricity for that."

"*Ach,* well, somehow Leah got a copy of the note because she obviously couldn't have written something like this at her age." Joseph refolded the letter and returned to Sadie.

As he lowered himself beside her, closer this time, on the couch, he cupped her cheek. "Do you think that you will ever be able to really trust me? I would never let harm come to you or Leah or any future *kinner* we might have."

Sadie grinned.

Joseph lowered his head. "Oops. Sorry. I guess that's moving too fast." But with his hand still on her cheek, he drew her lips to his, brushing against her slowly before he covered her mouth with his. "But I'm falling in *lieb* with you."

Sadie's knot in her throat began to dissolve. "I feel the same way," she said breathlessly. "But we can't have Leah believing I'm her new *mudder* when we are still discovering each other. And I have serious doubts that the bishop would approve of us moving forward as a family while you are technically still married."

"I know," Joseph said before he kissed her again. And again, and again. "But we have to talk to him."

"I knew it!" Leah came slowly into the room. She thrust both arms around her father and Sadie. "We are going to be a happy family."

For a child who had been through so much trauma, it was refreshing — and amazing — to see her resilience, and her tiny face was filled with such hope. Sadie chewed her lip and waited for Joseph to take the lead.

He eased his daughter away. "You can't just become a family overnight. It takes time, and there are things that would need approval from the bishop," Joseph said. "But I want you to go to bed, put this day behind you, and know that I will keep you safe for the rest of your life. I will come to tuck you in shortly, and we will give thanks and praise to *Gott.*"

"Maybe Sadie can tuck me in too." Leah's tiny face, still red from the earlier incident, lit up.

Sadie's heart warmed. "Of course I can do that."

She didn't know how Joseph would keep his promise to Leah — to keep her safe — since Grace had legal custody of Leah. Maybe she did end up calling the police. Or maybe Henry talked her out of that and talked some sense into her. She needed to talk to Henry to find out what had happened after they left. And to make sure he is safe.

After Leah hugged and kissed Sadie, Joseph walked her to the bedroom, and he stayed with her for a while. When he returned, he retook his position next to her on the couch. "She's a child. She doesn't understand how people fall in *lieb.*" He paused, grinning. "But I did ask her about the copy of this note we found in the drawer." Joseph held it up for a moment before lowering it back to his lap.

"She's been through so much, Joseph. I'm sure she needs some counseling. But did she explain about the note, who wrote it, and how she got a copy of it?"

"*Ya,* she did. And you were right all along. The day at the library, when we saw Lizzie and Esther, Lizzie was reading — or pretending to read — a book to Leah, and apparently that's when Lizzie wrote the letter. And they had a copy machine at the library. The sisters were convinced that none of the other men in the neighborhood were right for you, and that this new man . . ." He pointed to himself. ". . . just might be a perfect fit." He shook his head. "Which is crazy considering they didn't know me. But Leah said she told them all about me, leaving out the obvious things that I'd told her not to mention."

"So, it was Lizzie and Esther all along." Sadie thought back to her conversation with the elderly sisters, trying to decide if they had lied or just twisted the truth. If anyone could convince the bishop to make an exception to a divorce, it was probably Lizzie.

"Did they do *gut*?" Joseph kissed her again.

Sadie eased away, smiling. "Time will tell. But . . ." She reached down and held his hand. "How will you ever be free of Grace? She will continue to fight for Leah. What if she called the police? Couldn't they come and take Leah away? And the bishop probably won't allow dissolvement of the marriage. It's just not our way to divorce. Marriage is for life."

Joseph leaned into the couch cushions and began stroking his beard. "I've thought about that. I'd like to think she won't be back, but I also know the bishop is unlikely to approve of our relationship." He shook his head. "I don't want to always be looking over *mei* shoulder and fearful for Leah too."

"You won't be."

They both startled when they heard a gentle tap on the door. Henry pushed the screen door open. "Can I come in?"

"Ya," Joseph said as he quickly stood. "What happened after we left?"

Sadie rose, also, anxious to hear the outcome.

"I told Gretchen, or er — Grace — that we'd all testify at an English trial about what happened to Leah. She agreed to go back to Pennsylvania. And she promised to never come back."

Joseph shook Henry's hand. "*Danki.* I don't know how you convinced her to leave, but hopefully she will keep her word." He sighed. "Although keeping her word isn't something I'm sure she'll do."

"She will." Henry made the comment with such conviction that it was hard not to believe him. "And I'm not going to stay, but I knew you'd be worried about the outcome. I really don't think you will have to worry about Grace again."

They said their goodbyes, but Sadie had a niggling feeling. She held up one finger. "Joseph, I'll be right back."

Sadie flung open the door, rushed down the porch steps, and caught Henry before he got into his buggy. Breathless, she put a hand on his arm. "You paid her, didn't you?"

Henry looked down, kicked at the ground before he looked back at her. "It doesn't matter. She won't be back. I scribbled up an agreement, she signed it, and I told her again that we would testify against her."

Sadie pressed her lips together, sure that Henry had paid Grace not to come back. "I always knew you were a *gut* man, Henry."

He shrugged. "I try to be, but I certainly lost *mei* way when it came to Gretchen . . . I mean, Grace. I was inappropriate during the conversation we had at the school, and I behaved so badly by getting involved with Grace. I've asked *Gott* every day to forgive me."

Sadie touched his arm. "He forgave you

the first time you asked Him."

They were quiet for a few moments, then Henry locked eyes with Sadie. "I really hope things work out with you and Joseph. You deserve *lieb,* Sadie, and Joseph seems like a *gut* man. I hope the bishop will make an exception to Joseph's marriage and divorce so that the two of you can be together." He paused as he blinked his eyes a few times. "I don't want to be alone. I want someone special to share *mei* life with. I hope I can find *mei* perfect someone."

Sadie hugged him. "You will, Henry. I'm sure of it."

"I hope you're right." He tipped his hat in the near darkness as he walked to his buggy. "Take care."

As she stood beneath the propane lamp in the yard, two arms encircled her waist. "Do you think he's right, that Grace won't come back?"

"*Ya,* I believe he's correct." Sadie didn't want to keep anything from Joseph, but if Henry had paid Grace to leave — and Sadie was sure he did — he wouldn't want anyone to know.

"I think we need to go see Lizzie and Esther tomorrow." She turned to face him.

After he stole a quick kiss, he said, "Uh, oh. We aren't going to give them a hard time about writing the secret admirer note, are we?" He nibbled her ear until she giggled, and Sadie felt like a teenager, someone in love for the first time. "Because I think that our Leah working with Esther and Lizzie turned out to be a *gut* thing. I felt so protective of you right from the start that I knew I had to find out who wrote the note."

It warmed her heart to hear him say 'our Leah'. "*Nee,* I think things worked out exactly as *Gott* planned even if we can't see His long-term plan for us." She paused. "We will never be more than friends if the bishop doesn't make an exception."

It was harsh reality. Sadie sometimes wondered if she should have put a stop to their growing feelings for each other but turning Joseph away then or now felt heartbreaking.

He was quiet for a while, possibly pondering their outcome also.

"Then why the visit to see Esther and Lizzie? To thank them?" He sighed. "They must have a lot of faith in the bishop to overrule a long-standing belief that's clearly lined out in the *Ordnung.*

"I think we are going to have to trust *Gott* when it comes to our future, but I was thinking about paying the sisters a visit for another reason." She smiled, then waved at

Henry just before he turned the corner. "I do believe Esther and Lizzie have a new client. Henry."

Joseph laughed. "If anyone can help Henry find *lieb,* it's those two."

Lieb. Sadie had it for Joseph, and she felt it reverberating back at her.

In her heart, she knew she'd found her family. And she was sure the bishop would understand the circumstances and make an exception.

Epilogue

One year later . . .

Sadie tucked Leah into bed after reading her a story, then kissed her on the forehead before lowering the flame on her lantern.

Grace hadn't returned, and, over time, her absence had allowed Leah to heal and feel safe, along with some outside counseling that the bishop had approved. But things had been far from perfect. Bishop Graber was a stern older man who was not willing to bend when it came to the love Sadie and Joseph confessed to having for each other.

"Divorce is a violation of vows punishable by shunning," he'd told Joseph and Sadie.

While the bishop had allowed Joseph and Leah to stay in the community without forcing them to leave, he would not bless any romantic relationship between Sadie and Joseph, leaving the couple heartbroken and stuck in a friendship zone where neither of them could maneuver forward, but they remained united in another way — Leah's healing.

Sadie, Joseph, and Leah continued to share meals together, followed by devotions. Sometimes, Sadie cooked at her house, and other times Joseph made one of his specialties for the three of them. She realized that not every man was like her father, and her willingness to allow Joseph into her heart had blessed her in ways she couldn't have imagined. But every night, there were good-byes, and it was hard for Sadie not to feel cheated out of the life she'd never known she wanted.

Their unusual circumstances went on for three months, until word was sent that Grace had overdosed on pills. No one knew if her passing was intentional or an accident.

Leah felt a level of sadness and confusion, but time and youth helped her cope, along with the love Joseph and Sadie showered on her.

Grace's death was especially difficult for Sadie and Joseph, for reasons they admitted to each other and to the bishop. *Did I subconsciously will this to happen?*

Their guilt threw them into a tailspin for a while, but it was Bishop Graber who counseled them and relieved their inner turmoil, citing that things happen according to God's plan, not theirs.

A few months later, Sadie officially slipped into the role of Leah's mother after she and Joseph married. She still thought of Grace often and everything that the woman had lost — and Sadie had gained — but if guilt snuck up on her, she reminded herself that lives are defined by a combination of free will and God's plan.

Lizzie and Esther stayed busy. Henry was at the top of the sisters' matchmaking list, closely followed by Paul and Lloyd.

The sisters had their work cut out for them since their small community didn't offer many opportunities for them to play matchmaker, but that was not stopping Lizzie and Esther from stepping out into other districts in their efforts to find each man a happily-ever-after ending.

"Did she fall asleep during the story you read her?" Joseph asked, yawning, as Sadie walked into the living room. Her husband had tucked Leah in, then left the room when Sadie cuddled up with Leah to read her story. It had become their special time together.

"She is still awake, but I don't think she is far from sleep." Sadie sidled up next to Joseph on the couch and silently thanked the Lord — for the hundredth time — for blessing her with Joseph and Leah.

Joseph gently touched her stomach and smiled. "It's a boy, I think."

Sadie placed her hand on his, thinking how God's blessings hadn't stopped with just Joseph and Leah. "I think you're just wishing for a *sohn* to help you with the planting and harvest when he gets old enough."

Joseph chuckled. "Hmm . . ." He ran his other hand the length of his beard. "I hadn't thought of that."

Sadie playfully slapped him on the arm, knowing better.

"I will *lieb* him or her no matter what." He leaned over and kissed her. "We are so blessed."

Sadie's heart swelled as they both felt the baby moving. "More than we could have ever imagined."

Danki, Gott.

READING GROUP GUIDE

1. Sadie's background haunted her and left her untrusting of men. In what ways did she misidentify certain situations based on her childhood?

2. As Sadie introduced us to her list of "suspects/potential suitors", were you rooting for one of the men from the beginning? Did you foresee who would be Sadie's love interest?

3. Did you make the connection between Gretchen and Grace? If so, when?

4. Henry is a complicated character. Did you like or dislike him, and did your opinion of him change as the story progressed?

5. When Leah spilled her milk and Joseph reacted harshly, did you suspect him as being someone other than the way he portrayed himself? Did your opinion change, and could you relate to his frustrations and the way he blamed himself for certain things?

6. In the story, Sadie had preconceived opinions about each man. In what ways were her initial opinions incorrect? Was she being judgmental based on the only information she had? Did you fault her for this? Would you have assumed perceptions in the same way that Sadie did?

7. We are all guilty of judging a book by its cover. Can you recall a time when you judged a person before you knew what his or her true motivations were? If so, how was the situation resolved? Or was it?

8. Commonly, non-Amish couples have 'gender reveal' parties to find out if the baby is a boy or a girl. Do you think the Amish have these type of party?

9. If you could change any part of the story — without interrupting the overall plot — what would it be and why?

10. If you are a regular reader of Beth Wiseman's books, how does this story differ from her other novels?

AMISH RECIPES

Sadie's Cheeseball

2.5 packages of cream cheese (8.5 oz.) softened

4 oz. crumbled blue cheese

1 cup grated cheddar cheese

Small onion, finely diced

Combine the above ingredients, then form three balls and set aside.

On a plate, sprinkle finely chopped pecans, paprika, and dried parsley. Stir, then roll each ball in the mixture until completely coated.

Place on a square of Press N Seal (or something similar), completely cover the cheese ball, and put it in the refrigerator for at least two hours.

Joseph's Meatloaf

1 1/2 lb. ground beef

1/2 cup oats

1 small onion

Dash of Liquid Smoke
1 1/2 tsp. salt
1/4 tsp. pepper
1 egg, beaten
1/2 cup milk
1/2 cup tomato juice
Mix all of the above at 350 for 1 1/2 hours. Top with the following sauce and enjoy!
1/3 cup ketchup
1 T. mustard
1 T. brown sugar

Chicken Noodle Bake

3 T. melted butter
1/2 onion (medium), diced
1 cup Velveeta cheese, shredded
1 1/2 cups milk
1 can cream of mushroom soup
1 pt. chicken broth
1/4 tsp. pepper
1 1/2 tsp. salt
1 (8 oz.) package raw noodles or 2 cups macaroni, uncooked
Mix all of the above together, except noodles/macaroni — add them last.
Bake, uncovered 1 1/2 hours at 350. Stir a few times while baking.

Hot Pepper Butter

42 hot peppers
1 pt. yellow mustard
1 qt. vinegar
6 cups sugar
1 T. salt
1 cup flour
1 1/2 cup water

Grind hot peppers and add mustard, vinegar, sugar, and salt. Bring to a boil. Make a paste with the flour and water. Add to boiling mixture and cook for 5 minutes. Pour into pints and seal. Makes 7 pints.

Butter Pecan Bars

2 eggs, beaten
1 cup brown sugar
1 cup white sugar
3/4 cup melted butter
1/2 tsp. soda
1 1/4 cup flour
1 cup chopped pecans
dash of vanilla

Mix eggs, sugars, and butter; add flour, soda, nuts, and vanilla. Mix well and pour into lightly greased 9″×13″ pan. Bake at 350 for 30-40 minutes. Cut into squares or bars while still warm. Inside will be moist.

ACKNOWLEDGMENTS

It's always been said that it takes a village to publish a book, and I completely agree. I wouldn't be able to continue my love of writing if not for my 'villagers' — many of whom I've had on my team for years.

A big thanks to my editors, Audrey Wick and Janet Murphy. You gals keep me on my toes, for sure. I am able to put out better books because of your keen insight and expertise. Love you both.

I have an amazing street team — Wiseman's Warriors. These wonderful ladies are also part of my village, the marketing suburb. Thanks for all you do to get my books seen and read!

To my family and friends who continue to support me after all these years, I love you forever.

As always, God gets the credit for every story He bestows on my heart. Thank you, Lord.

ABOUT THE AUTHOR

Bestselling and award-winning author **Beth Wiseman** has sold over 3 million books. She is the recipient of the coveted Holt Medallion, a two-time Carol Award winner, and has won the Inspirational Reader's Choice Award three times. Her books have been on various bestseller lists, including CBD, CBA, ECPA, and *Publishers Weekly*. Beth and her husband are empty nesters enjoying country life in south central Texas.

The employees of Thorndike Press hope you have enjoyed this Large Print book. All our Thorndike Large Print titles are designed for easy reading, and all our books are made to last. Other Thorndike Press Large Print books are available at your library, through selected bookstores, or directly from us.

For information about titles, please call:
(800) 223-1244

or visit our website at:
gale.com/thorndike